Wallwave the Young Sea Warrior
ADVENTURES OF WAR QUEENS AND BATTLE HEROES

In the days before written history, clues to everyday events can be found of the existence of a chariot-based civilization in the Western Plains of Russia and Mongolia. This points to a way of life based on chariots, horses and bronze-age weapons. These clues include aerial sites, chariots, jewelry, swords and axes. Evidently the charioteers lived, died and were buried in a horse-based way of life that was more advanced in terms of chariots that had been developed up to that time.

This civilization had apparently covered much of the Asian and Chinese as well as the Russian Western Plains. It was a pre-Celtic way of life. We do not know the name of the tribes or what language they spoke. The islands and rivers had not yet been taken over by Vikings, as happened later. How did a pre-Viking and pre-Celtic civilization develop into the later domination of the Vikings which was spread throughout eastern Europe and western Asia and Russia?

Obviously, pre-Gaelic and pre-Viking legends and myth need to be consulted. The longboats of war as well as chariots play a powerful part in these adventures. In those days warrior queens as well as heroic Vikings played a large part.

The latter-day wars organized by Queen Bodicea of Britain who drove the Romans out of the British Isles; Queen Maeve of Connaught who led the united armies of Ireland against Ulster were similarly heroic figures. These warrior queens were field-marshals and planners of war as well as chariot warriors. Perhaps the last of this line was Saint Joan of Arc.

In WALLWAVE THE YOUNG SEA WARRIOR, the story covers his birth, boyhood and early life with his father King Waterbear and his mother War Queen Springvision.

Wallwave the Young Sea Warrior
BOYHOOD AND SEABIRDS

This book describes the supernatural origins of Wallwave and the struggles of his father King Waterbear to overcome the attacks of the western powers of darkness.

LIFE OF DREW CARSON

Sam Drew Carson was born in the North of Ireland and educated there at Wellington College and the Ulster Polytechnic. He completed his education in the USA at New Mexico Highlands University and the University of Arkansas and has traveled widely in North America, around the Atlantic and in Europe.

Drew worked as a seaman and fish-gutter in Vestmannaeyjar off the coast of Iceland. He lived and worked in the Irish and Western Isles Gaeltachts and was married in Welsh-speaking Carmarthen after which he honeymooned in Belfast. He has told his stories, composed and sung his songs, seeking storylines in Bristol and the English Westcountry. Drew has also lived and written in Nashville, Tennessee, in the wooded hills of Mid-America and from the Appalachians to the Ozarks. This was the culture that gave rise to the now worldwide Scotch-Irish country music.

In the USA, he also worked beside the bayous of the French-speaking Cajuns in the South and among the Western Spanish-speaking Navajos, Apaches and Pueblos of the Sangre de Cristo Mountains in New Mexico.

Drew has sailed far into the seas of old Gaelic and Oriental legend. After many years searching for inspiration for story and music, the author is still traveling and writing.

BOOKS BY THE SAME AUTHOR

ZENISUB
Fun and Games in Businezz
ISBN: 978-0-9561435-2-5

GOOD FOR A LAUGH
Six Funny Playscripts for Amateurs
ISBN: 978-0-9561435-3-2

HOME WITH A GOOD COMPANION
Amateur Pantomime Scripts for a Merry Winter
ISBN: 978-0-9561435-4-9

CLASSIC EUROPEAN LYRICS
Translated from the Gaelic, the French and Spanish
ISBN: 978-0-9561435-6-3

COMMONWEALTH
An Introduction to Business Economics
ISBN: 978-0-9561435-7-0

MISSING PERSONS
Detective Felix O'Neill in a Crime Adventure
ISBN: 978-0-9561435-8-7

WEREWOLF MURDERS
Detective Felix O'Neill in a Crime Adventure
ISBN: 978-0-9561435-9-4

ORIENTAL GOVERNESS
Detective Felix O'Neill in a Crime Adventure
ISBN: 978-1-908184-00-9

LOOKING BACK
Four Nostalgic Playscripts for Amateurs
ISBN: 978-1-908184-01-6

EASTER AND THE SPRINGTIME
Five Amateur Playscripts about New Life
ISBN: 978-1-908184-02-3

WALLWAVE THE YOUNG SEA WARRIOR
Adventures of War Queens and Battle Heroes
ISBN: 978-1-908184-03-0

WALLWAVE THE SEA PRINCE
Adventures of War Queens and Battle Heroes
ISBN: 978-1-908184-04-7

WALLWAVE THE SEA KING
Adventures of War Queens and Battle Heroes
ISBN: 978-1-908184-05-4

Wallwave the Young Sea Warrior
Adventures of War Queens
and Battle Heroes

BY
DREW CARSON

Order from:
https://www.createspace.com/3965988

Legals

ISBN: 978-1-908184-03-0

CONTENTS

CONTENTS

MAIN CHARACTERS IN THE ADVENTURES OF WALLWAVE

SEAGULL HEROES – THE WAVEWARRIORS
Waterbear, *King of Seagulls, an oriental warrior. Rider of the Great White Stallion (a horse with white hair and mane)*
Seaspear, *admiral of the Hillwolves fleet, a fieldmarshal of the sea of Wavewarrior origin*
Stormleaper, *a hero of many battles*
Whaleroarer, *a hero of fierce combats*
Icedragon, *a hero and fieldmarshal deputy*
Summersailor, *vice-king and fieldmarshal supreme, head of Hawks battalion*
Shadowhero, *great uncle and trainer of the young Wallwave and Stormbolt*
*Wallwave, *oriental youth, son of Waterbear*
Stormbolt, *younger son of Waterbear*

HILLWOLVES
Warchariot, *King of Hillwolves*
Sternrider, *supreme fieldmarshal and commander in chief of Hillwolves. Rider of the Great Bay Horse of the West*
Winterwarrior, *deputy fieldmarshal and next in command of the Hillwolves*

* also known as Tsunami

Main Characters

Winterfire, *the son of Winterwarrior*
Oakhill, *an assassin*
Cragfox, *in charge of shoreline defenses*
Flyingbat, *brother of Oakhill*
Abbott Ratrunner, *a monk who breeds rats*

The Deathhead Dwarfs, *four-eyed assassins*
The Killer Disguisers, *chamelion-like killers*

Hillwolf Queens

Queen Snakeknife, *queen of Warchariot*
Queen Spiderlair, *Warchariot's ancient mother*
Queen of Justice, *a sycophant, a false omenteller*
Queen Rainbow, *Snakeknife's mother*

Seagull Queens

Springvision, *queen of Waterbear. She has the gifts of magic and spells and discernment of spirits*
Gentleleaf, *loyal queen of Seaspear*
Whitehair, *young niece of Summersailor*
Purplelake, *sister of Summersailor*
Maplewine, *queen to Whaleroarer*
Willowflame, *queen to Icedragon*
Streamflower, *queen to Stormleaper*

MAIN CHARACTERS

FOUR WITCHES OF KILL
Windweasel, *of the air*
Rivershark, *of the waters*
Meteoreyes, *of fire and hills*
Landslink, *of soil and earth*

TWO STALLIONS
Oceanhorse, *the Great White Stallion of the East*
Foresthorse, *the Great Bay Stallion of the West*

SUPERNATURALS
Truthteller, *Master of good words*
Old Washerwoman, *Diviner of omens*
Mooncrow, *a spy-bird of war*
Red Warriorwoman, *teller of fortunes*
Bullaxe, *ugly ogre with magic powers*
Firefiend, *a man of flames*
Tear, Sigh, Smile, Laugh, *Queens from Islands of the Everyoung*

COMBAT PERSONA
Salmon of Wisdom
Wine of Vision
*Shield of Roar, gives warning
*Bonespear, thirsts for blood
*Hardblade, a rainbow sword
magic weapons that occasionally appear

CHAPTER ONE

STALLIONS – THE WHITE AND THE BAY

Who is the tyrant of seas, hills and plains? Who is the sovereign of the air and clouds? Black Weather is the tyrant of the world - brutal and vicious, screaming and unruly, setting up savage storms on the sea of green weed and undulating hills of swirling foam. Weather tears up the trees on the high hills and fries the fields with fire, kills the small creatures, burns down the barns, crushes and floods the farmhouse. Weather is the eternal master of the forests and the ocean and the sky.

At one time Weather delegated its turmoil into the strength of two great stallions – a Bay and a White - to jointly rule the earth, its men and armies. These two great stallions were given power like two fieldmarshals over their herds to rule and lead wild horses on the moors.

The White, Oceanhorse, the Great White Stallion of the East, was the stallion of the waves born out of the sea storms of the ice.

The Bay, Foresthorse, the Great Bay Stallion of the West, was the leader of the hills, being born out of the steaming jungles and forests, sprung from the lightning strikes of the brown earth out of the fire and soil. His mane and tail were black, his skin was brown and shiny red. His name was Foresthorse, named for the jungles from which he had emerged in the fire and lightning.

The White was the chariot horse of brave Waterbear, the ruler of the seagull Wavewarriors.

The Bay was the chariot horse of Warchariot and Snakeknife, king and queen of the Hillwolves and their fieldmarshal, Sternrider.

These horses had the powerful intellect almost of men, especially in ways of war. They were adept at rounding up wild horses and driving them into their combat camps. There they were embattled, tamed and trained in warfare and in all the skills of courage, sidestepping, plunging and fine footwork of charioteering.

One day in summer, the Great Bay invaded the eastern moors and rounded up six foals, driving them back to where the straits divided the East islands from the West islands of the world.

At the same time, the White reared up and neighed and plunged his forehooves high into the air, escaping and galloping from his charioteer. Then he dashed along the wide highway that led to the straits separating the two lands.

When Waterbear and his fair Queen Springvision saw the Great White escaping, Springvision wept because she loved the White.

And Seaspear, brother of Springvision and friend of Waterbear for many years, along with Gentleleaf, the queen of Seaspear, all set out on the road to catch the White.

Seaspear was tall and straight, fair-haired, blue-eyed – the fiercest combat warrior of the Seagulls, skilled in the ways of waves and seas and boats, next only to the King, brave Waterbear.

Springvision was the Queen of the Waterbear. Known for her sharp eyesight and true wisdom. She also acted as his councilor. Gentleleaf was the loyal Queen of Seaspear.

As they sped off, Springvision dried her tears – she was a warriorwoman who loved great horses.

"He is my horse – a hero of the field . . . Oceanhorse is our leader who goes before us."

Springvision spoke in a quiet and thoughtful way, "Only a horse has all the qualities that go to make up true nobility. A horse is gentle, sensitive and strong. A horse is proud and delicate yet difficult to master or subdue. A stallion is an earl, a viceking, an admiral of the moors. Only man is the master of the horse – no other animal could stand before it. If we should lose our horses, we lose all. Horses and ladies, olderfolk and our children would all be taken over by the Hillwolves. Even our boats, those horses of the sea, would have no place to berth if we should lack harbors and havens protected by our stallions set in their chariots, those jeweled wicker thrones of war.

"The horse is not a crude machine of battle, it has great dignity and decency of spirit. It is not petty minded or quick to change. The horse is a true noble surrounded by long knives lurking to kill. All the great warriors of old rode on a horse. Many of the great fieldmarshals of war rode on a horse or posed astride its back − proud to be seen in charge and in the saddle. For the horse imparts its own nobility and its own calm control to the horserider. The hero is the man on the white horse. For true nobility does not come from acclaim or from the approbation of a vi-king. Rather, nobility surges from within like a wallwave of the inner spirit. All horses have this spirit of nobility but the great stallions of the world have also a splendid gentility and courage. These are the qualities seen in our own White, the Oceanhorse and the Great Bay Stallion, the Foresthorse of our western neighbors. Truly I love them both but the Great Bay is far too good and honest to serve either Snakeknife or Warchariot."

Then Seaspear told the story of the stallions, "These stallions have a pedigree of spirit charged and immersed in all the ways of war. I have heard from the songwriters and storytellers of their great transformations in the past from one form to another of enmity. Great as these fighting stallions are today, they have taken the form of smaller combatants in times past. They have grown and matured over the centuries.

"The tyrant Weather – the fierce spirit of conquest and destruction – has seeped into their many successive forms. Long centuries before they were born into the world as other creatures, but in whatever form, they always brought about death and destruction.

"First, they were crias diving into the sea and swooping down upon the heads of men. The men fought back with swords and killed the crias, then fell to arguing and blaming each other, finally coming to blows and fighting duels. When the crias were killed they were reborn as crows soaring above the hills and waterfalls, cawing and calling out to insult each other. The insults fell on the ears of demented men who slew the men of other tribes and clans and once again bitter battles were fought.

"Once more the two warspirits were reborn as buzzards of the bush and dusty plains. Slowly and sinisterly they flew above the dried-up fields that screamed for streams and water. Meanly they picked among the bones of those who lay dying and drying in the sun.

"'Leave us alone' the still-alive cried out 'and let us bury our dead with decency.' Then they took to blaming each other for the buzzards and hacked and hewed and stabbed their fellow farmers in a great war over the streams and waters. 'There – you can be buzzard meat' they told each other. Then men turned on the two buzzards and slew them.

"The third time they were reborn as speckled hawks who fly into the sky and then swoop down to sink their claws into the necks of men. Again the men cried out to other men, 'control your hawks or we will take their heads.' But soon the men were taking off the heads of other men. The hawks flew far away and tore each other apart far in the jungle.

"Now the Mooncrow, the ugly haggard crone of war, has flown above their bones and stirred them up so that the two war spirits have been reborn as powerful stallions – a White horse and a Bay – each with the blood of Weather in his veins. Now they will try to use tumult and turmoil and we must not be misled by these stallions into a war that would destroy both sides. For the Mooncrow, the haggard witch of war, who lives among the rafters of the rich, will always strike both victor and defeated."

Springvision nodded to agree with Seaspear, "In war let both winner and loser beware. So let the Great White Stallion of the East be kept apart from the Great Bay of the West. For the White will not stand for theft of horses and stallions or mares or colts by the Great Bay. It is said that in all the world there is no equal to these great horses."

Waterbear spoke up, "It is known that both great stallions are the leaders of all the other horses of the moors. If one of these horses, the White or the Bay, is angered, he will snort and bellow fire like a green dragon or like thunder pounding and galloping throughout the land. The White would trample into the ground any intruders who dared approach him in his anger. We need to pump cold water on the White until he calms down – if we wish to harness him. When he is running free, he prances and marches ahead of the other horses – they follow him as he holds high his head above broad shoulders like any king in a victory procession. His hooves are pure gold laid over iron."

After an hour following its tracks, they found the White reared up and attacking the Bay. The Bay was trying to herd away six of the eastern foals over the isthmus. Waterbear shot a slingstone and grazed the Bay, frightening it away.

The Bay plunged over the spraying water and kicked fine sprays of fountains of the saltsea foam. It fled from the stolen foals and whinnied, as many creatures of the sea and air flew up and flew around – crias and crows and buzzards and high hawks.

CHAPTER TWO
STORMS OF WAR

On the eastern side of the isthmus, the Great White Stallion Oceanhorse was now safely returned to King Waterbear and his Queen Springvision.

The four Wavewarriors in their chariots – brave Waterbear, Seaspear and the warriorwomen Springvision and Gentleleaf – watched as Foresthorse returned to join Sternrider, the senior fieldmarshal of the Hillwolves, who was waiting on the western side of the straits.

Springvision had the youngest and best eyes. She stared into the distance and told her husband and her brother all the far sights she could see.

"I see a cold storm of freezing rain and sleet as sharp as any forest of long spears. It seems to cut the faces of two warriors and the back of the great Bayhorse shudders and shakes. What is the meaning of that great icestorm?"

Waterbear answered, "That is the sleet of hell, the hail of slaughter, now being stirred up by Sternrider among his armies, to unleash upon his foes. He is always planning some far away attack along with his deputy fieldmarshal, the Winterwarrior who both have hearts of ice."

Springvision looked again and saw low fog lying on the plains far into the distance, just like the misty pall that drapes a palace, when a king draws near to home on a snowy day.

Springvision asked, "What is that low white fog far, far away?"

"That fog," Seaspear spoke up, "on the far plains, is the heavy breath of warriors and horses, belonging to King Warchariot and his queen, gathering together and milling all around as they rally and host on the western plains. No doubt that is just an exercise of war, a military game to train the troops."

Waterbear watched as Foresthorse fled away. Then Sternrider, the fieldmarshal of the Hillwolves, came out from behind thick trees, bridled Foresthorse and handed the horse over to his deputy, Winterwarrior, to harness the horse and yoke him to their chariot. The two fieldmarshals climbed aboard and drove off. Their chariot was like a ship in the green fields or a moving throne upon the battlefield.

Suddenly the air was filled with flying ravens above the heads of the fieldmarshal's chariot.

Springvision saw the birds fly up and caw – circling around the chariot. "I see blackbirds – a flock of ravens – flying above the chariot. They fly up high into the clouds above."

Springvision asked the king, "What are those ravens?"

"Those are not ravens," said the Waterbear. "Those are the sods of black earth thrown up high by the hooves of the Great Bay as he sets off."

Suddenly a chariot, driven by two great horses, broke out of the misty pall and came to meet the chariot of the Bay and the two fieldmarshals. The charioteer stood high behind the hood, manipulating the reins with dexterous skill, well clear of the snorts and breathings and foamings, sweats and smells of the two great chariot horses. This coming chariot was the royal coach. It was well sprung and floated with great ease over the long green fields towards the straits.

The horses were both of the same size and shape – one black, the other gray, sturdy and swift, equal in clean groomed beauty and hair brushing. Their harnesses were leather and gold and silver studded with precious gems, rubies and diamonds.

Their hooves and backs were broad and strong and clean. They pranced, high-stepping proudly in unison like soldiers in a phalanx, step-in-step together as they pulled the moving throne, swaying and singing on its powerful wheels. The horses were both large, of the same height, prancing with great intensity and strength. Their heads were small, sharply intelligent. Their lips were large. Their eyes were bright. Their chests were ruddy, sleek and smoothly groomed, as they bowed their necks in lofty dignity and yielded instantly to the reins and yoke. Their manes and tails flowed free in long black curls.

The broad chariot was built of yew and wicker with seats set back within a hood of blue. The reins were studded with colored gems and gold. The chariot's shafts were smooth and strong, as hard as spears and the central pole was ringed around with bronze. The silver yoke was light and flexible.

Inside the chariot sat a giant warrior with thick black hair and beard as smooth as silk. His eyes were grey and flashed backward and forward as he took note of the chariot of his fieldmarshals and searched the distant shoreline of the straits.

Around him flowed a purple cloak of linen with white-laced fringes. This great cloak was held in place by a bright broach of silver and the folds of the cloak swept back across his shoulders beside the wide blue hood. Across his knees there lay a golden hilted sword of steel. In his right hand he held up a broad spear with a thin shaft of ash. In his left hand he held a deadly dagger at the ready.

Slung over his broad shoulders was a shield with orle of silver all around the rim. Across the purple shield there was embossed a ring of running foxes, wolves and stags. His savage teeth were sparkling and bright flashing out from thick lips of blackberry and red. His brows were brooding over his piercing eyes like two great shaggy bears in a black forest.

Beside him in the chariot stood his queen – slender and tall but muscular and tense. She whipped along the two proud chariot horses with a whip of thin and flexible red leather. Her arms and face were freckled, brown with sun. Her hair was long and red and flowing wild – held back in place with a gold band on her forehead to stop the hair from falling over her eyes. Behind her ears were two broad rings of gold and into these her red hair had been gathered. She wore a two-sleeved light cloak over four studded leather strengtheners for her wrists and ankles, along with a shield, a sword, a javelin and a dagger. Like a true warriorwoman in the field, she tensed the muscles of her arms and legs to balance herself for the rolling of the chariot.

Soon the fine chariot drove off and left the two fieldmarshals in the chariot pulled by the Bay.

Waterbear explained to Springvision his queen, "That was Warchariot and his warrior queen Snakeknife of the cunning lies and murders. I am his step-brother. When my mother, Queen Silvercheek died, my father King Snowcurl, married the witch Spiderlair. She cheated my father out of giving the Kingdom to me. Now I rule only half of the great Kingdom that was land and sea. The other half is ruled by her son, the Warchariot whose father was a thief who lived in darkness.

"Warchariot and Snakeknife had come to parley and plot with their fieldmarshals to hear how their Great Bay Stallion made out in his exploratory foray among our horses. Perhaps this little horse trick was a test to find out if the omens were fortuitous."

Springvision said, "Perhaps that was the case but a dark gray cloud hung over the brief meeting and rain and sleet poured from the unfriendly skies, cutting the faces, almost shaving the head of the king or queen and the two fieldmarshals."

Springvision saw the dark clouds hanging over them and watched as they turned their chariot and sped to their own troops, still draped in a misty pall.

Just at this time the Great Bay turned around. Sternrider stood up in his chariot and looked back to the straits where Seaspear stood with Gentleleaf, his queen. There also stood Waterbear and the warrior queen, Springvision. Sternrider, ever polite and diplomatic, then drove off after turning to salute and bow to Waterbear, as the king of all the Seagulls. And Waterbear solemnly returned the greeting.

Then the brave Waterbear addressed Springvision, Seaspear and Gentleleaf, "I fear that we will hear more from the fieldmarshal. For now the four divisions of our army have been disturbed and thrown up in the air in symbols of our foursquare war battalions. Sternrider has shown us his cunning lies in hiding his own skin and lurking back. His mount, Foresthorse, tests out our state of wariness and watchfulness. This cools my neck and makes me wonder what sly tricks he may be hiding up ahead. These tricks apply both to Sternrider and his deputy, the Winterwarrior."

Crias and crows, buzzards and hawks rose up out of their trees and crags and rocky ledges, fleeing in fear of the stomping of the horses.

Waterbear spoke of fate to the wise Springvision.

"Surely this is an omen," said Queen Springvision, "a trial run, a foray to steal horses for chariots - the moving thrones of war. Without them we would be helpless on our feet and the enemy could cut us down like grass. And yet, the omen foretells much in our favor, for the Bay has gone home without the stolen foals."

Springvision calmed the White, the Oceanhorse and harnessed him. "We know you were trying to chase off the Bay, but later, Oceanhorse - after great battles. Each of those seabirds represent an army that swirls around and turmoils. There is the cria of the seas and sandy shorelines. There is the crow that soars over high hills and perches with tight claws on crags and waterfalls and dizzy cliffs. There is the buzzard of the bushes and the plains and finally, there is the hawk that rises up high into the sky and pierces all things below him with sharp eyes."

And Seaspear spoke to Waterbear, his friend, "I see, brave Waterbear, that without horses an army cannot go to face a foe. But we have great fieldmarshals who are champions. They are decked in full armor with the accoutrements and swords of every kind of martial art. They have skills ready to team together and defend the horses of the East from the thieving hands of Sternrider and his army of horsethieves and not least, we have a fleet of many ships."

The King, brave Waterbear, replied, "We have you on our side Seaspear, as admiral of the ships. We also have you, my brother in battle, here to help us and advise us along with your assistant Stormleaper of the waters. There is Whaleroarer of the dizzy waterfalls. We have Icedragon who can cut through a phalanx of keen warriors like a butcher's knife and the Summersailor, fieldmarshal of Sky, who rages into a killfury combat when he comes face-to-face with any enemy. His niece, Whitehair, is a young girl of vision and wisdom. We could do worse than ask her for the omens."

But Gentleleaf worried, "There must be some plots still to steal our horses and disarm us."

Then Seaspear waved his hand, making light of all his queen's deep worries, "It's only Sternrider trying to steal a few foals – it's not an invasion. He could not even succeed in stealing foals."

Gentleleaf frowned, "One thing leads to another. I could not hear what the Queen Snakeknife and King Warchariot said to their fieldmarshals but the black weather of storm interpreted. I see a storm of bloodshed on the horizon. I tell you friend will murder friend. Good husbands will desert their loyal wives for the other woman Death. Blood will fall like sharp rain from the sky. Swords and knives will sleet like winter storms. Pillars of loyalty will desert their comrades and corpses will inherit fertile lands to rot and fester in those lands forever."

And wise Springvision agreed with Gentleleaf, "No. This is no simple matter. I do not think that we can make light of the Bay's intrusion. It is easy to ride two horses at the same time when they are riding side by side. But not when they are charging together head on head. You need to ride on one side or the other. You cannot span a war. It is too devious. There are too many subtle shades of combat not only to your chosen side for winning but to your relatives and friends and cousins. That is why a war divides the comrades, father and son and even brother and sister. Though there are standards of honor, skill and courage, there is no such thing as a just and honest war. All wars are cesspits of tumult and turmoil. Only the forces of nature ever win. That meeting of the Hillwolves was an omen."

Then Waterbear and Seaspear along with Springvision and Gentleleaf returned to the distant fastness of the Wavewarriors, a cool and snowy island of deep caves.

Then the Waterbear dwelt in the seasworld depths and sat upon his throne on the high roof from time to time. His garments glittered in gold and bronze and pale sunlight in blustery and salty breezes from the sea.

CHAPTER THREE
THE FOUR WITCHES

The four witches lived in a castle with the Mooncrow. This keep was known as Warwords Hostelry where the unwary traveler was lured away into the spells and visions of the witches.

The Four Witches of Kill crawled in their lair deep among cobwebs – the place of spiders.

Windweasel clutched the air with sharp wrinkled claws and sneered with her toothless mouth.

Meteroeyes had eyes like burning flames, a head as bald as stone, and a warted mouth that twisted tightly closed.

Landslink was a wrinkled, wizened and gaunt old crone with blackened sharp teeth like burnt-out embers.

Rivershark was a daughter of the tomb, now kept alive only by spells and potions that stoked the flames of life in the living dead. Her skin was like a dried-up withered seal skin.

***

Then King Warchariot, his wife Snakeknife and their two fieldmarshals, Sternrider and Winterwarrior went to seek war wisdom from the Witches of Kill.

The Four Witches of Kill greeted King Warchariot and his group. Warchariot and Sternrider wore the purple robes of high birth.

Snakeknife asked the witches, "What are the omens for this coming war?"

The witches told Snakeknife, "There are omens a-plenty but we have powers to help you win, whether the time was right or wrong, whether the omens tell of a defeat or a great victory."

The king and queen asked the four witches how they could win a war against the Wavewarriors with as few casualties and deaths as possible.

One of the witches, Landslink, told the chief fieldmarshal, Sternrider and his deputy Winterwarrior, to avoid a bloodbath where most of their best warriors would die. They should command and so control Seaspear, the greatest warrior and seaman of the Wavewarriors. As for the other heroes of the Seagulls, their four great fieldmarshals and champions would soon be sent away to live abroad. For the witches would conjure up the beckoning ghosts to lead them to the otherworld of dreams.

Then the four witches set up their battle plan and stared into the flames and flares to see what images would emerge out of the fire. These wrinkled, wizened and gaunt old crones plotted together. These four vile daughters of the tomb clawed deadly fingers and were kept alive only by magic potions and strange foods and pills of doctors skilled in mindmadness and delusion.

Then Landslink spoke to the Sternrider, "If Seaspear changes sides and joins you, this would leave only one void. The Wavewarriors also have their four great fieldmarshals: Summersailor, Icedragon, Whaleroarer and Stormleaper. They could not be removed with head-on combat for they are surrounded by their heroes and champions. They need to be distracted from the battle and we have many powers to lure them.

"Summersailor is the brother of King Waterbear and leads the great division of the sky where warriors fly like hawks to bring warhelp to all their fellows where help is needed most in the fierce, furious clashes on the field.

"Icedragon is the fieldmarshal of plains and low bushlands - the home of the gray buzzard.

"Where crias scream and swoop and soar in anger, there is Whaleroarer, champion of the hills, the mountains and the cliff-high waterfalls, where the black crows fly and dominate the night.

"Stormleaper is a hero of many battles who leaps above the tyrants of the storm."

Then the Meteoreyes spoke up, "Queen Springvision has the power of discernment of spirits. She visits everywhere in the castle of Waterbear. She could very easily dissolve the screen of our visions and then banish the Queens of the Everyoung back to their western isles. But we will bring clear visions to each hero at home in his own fastness -

free of all the crude interference from Springvision's powers."

Windweasel looked into the flames and spoke, "The lands and harbors of the Wavewarriors, in the absence of their fieldmarshals and heroes, can be invaded by your Hillwolf armies and you can drive away their herds of horses. They will be left with empty chariots, horseless moors and corrals with no warhorses and also empty stables. Their boats would only be able to engage other boats - for boats cannot prevail on the dry land. Seaspear will never send his newfound fleet of Wolves in boats to fight with his own Seagulls. This leaves only Waterbear to stand alone against a wild world of aggressors. And what can one man do against an army when he has only rabble and old men to fight for him? The Seagulls will be left with Waterbear and only this one great champion to fight for them.

Then Rivershark reminded the king and queen, "We have the wisdom and power of the Four Witches of Kill. The four battalions make up a fighting force that covers all the needs of any invasion – here all the arts of warfare are well met.

However, such an army can surely be wiped out by a balanced foe when there is missing from the fields and seas of battle the four fieldmarshals of the crias, crows, buzzards and seahawks, who represent the four fronts in a war.

"Therefore, control or influence the Seaspear and leave it to our false visions to distract the four fieldmarshals. Only the Waterbear will totter and struggle alone against our armies. Oh! Watch and see how one man fails and flounders who stands alone against our combined forces.

"For you will have seized the horses of the Seagulls, leaving them only empty chariots rotting and falling apart and rusting over in the cold, wet, wintry place that they call home. Drive in and take their foods and land, craftsmen, ladies with ornaments of gold and gems and all their homes from palaces to farms."

And the Four Witches of Kill pledged that they would also lure away, far over the sea to the land of youth, the four great heroes of Wavewarriors with all their followers and entourages.

"Finally," said Windweasel, "When the Seagull heroes have been lured away by the Hillwolves, it would be time to invade the eastern lands and take over their undefended homes. "

Sternrider and Winterwarrior also asked advice from the four witches but were not as worried about the signs and prophecies.

All sat in the dark Castle of Warwords and drank the dark red wine of battle vision and ate the eels of wily, cunning schemes.

Windweasel said, "There is one great stallion on either side. Each stallion pulls the chariot of the great warriors of the Seagulls and Hillwolves. Each stallion leads the horse herds of both sides and rules above the other colts and stallions like a great warlord of the hills and moors. If we enchant the heroes of the Seagulls, sending them far away, then you, Sternrider, can herd the horses of the Wavewarriors to your side. When the great heroes of the Wavewarriors return, they will come back to rusted chariots and without horses they can only perish."

And Snakeknife and the Warchariot counseled themselves that once the four heroes of the Wavewarriors would have been enchanted to the western isles it would be easy to seize and hold a hostage, perhaps a near and dear one of the Waterbear.

The Four Witches laid out the greater strategy.

"We also need a Seer of Win to lift the hearts and minds of all those on your side to encourage and build up the hope of winning among our main warriors and servants. The Queen of Justice is a false teller of omens who is easily bribed to predict a Hillwolf victory."

So the four witches planned and schemed together to hire a Seagull of a high rank (perhaps Seaspear) who would earn the respect of all other Seagulls. Then they would call upon the Powers of Win through the enchantment of the Four Witches of Kill.

The four witches chose the hiring of Seaspear for he was a warrior who could not be conquered by any foe. He was more swift and deadly than anyone but Waterbear. Seaspear fought with a heart of stone and an arm of threshing steel.

The Four Witches of Kill agreed with Snakeknife to find good omens for their secret war plans.

"Yes we can set the strategy of Win but we are witches not brave warriorwomen or fightingmen who must fight in the field in one-to-one fierce battles, day-to-day. We will support you all we can – never fear."

***

So Warchariot and Snakeknife, along with their two fieldmarshals, returned then to their war fortress on the plains of chariots.

At their fastness, a tall young woman stood before their gaze. Her hair was black, her eyes and skin were red. She wore a flowing cloak of red around her. Each of her eyes had red pupils within them. She wore two shoes with buckles of red gold. Around her long face hung two soft black tresses. Her long black eyelashes cast a shadow upon each cheek, making her face seem broad across the eyes and narrower at the chin. Her lips were like strawberries and her teeth were white and glistening like deep-sea pearls. Her chariot was drawn by two black horses and all around them was an aura of night.

Snakeknife asked the woman in the black chariot, "My armies are now hosting; will they win?"

"I am the Red Warriorwoman – a seer. I see only a haze of red upon your armies – a fog of misty blood floats over their heads."

Snakeknife asked the dark, young seer again, "In any assembly of young men and warriors there are bound to be manly fights among themselves. Many will come to blows and shed red blood. Look once again, young seer, what do you see?"

"I see a mist of red, a crimson fog."

"No, No." Warchariot cried, "This is mistaken – you do not understand. In a huge hosting, a great assembly like our mighty army, there are bound to be many, even among the victors, who will die in triumph and be held in honor. Take a new look at the final outcome. Now, tell me what do you see – success or failure?"

The young prophetic woman with the gift of second sight replied, "I see red blood. I see a mighty warrior from the lakes and snow plains of the East. He is a water warrior who will destroy your army like a tempest tearing down shrubs and plants and trees and bushes, slaughtering all before him like a lion ripping through squealing monkeys in a cage. He is like a shark cutting and swallowing small fish and tiny creatures of the sea."

Snakeknife was furious and reached for her javelin. "Liar," she screamed.

But Warchariot said, "No, do not bring any more bad luck upon us. Let us improve our armies to the point where they will all be sure to overwhelm. Let us get more wisdom from the four old witches who always bring good luck to any army. The four who have mastered the cold arts of kill and who have schemes and plots and devious magic that will ensure success."

The young seer sneered at the Snakeknife and drove off in anger.

"Yes," agreed Snakeknife, "let us wait until the time is right to go to war, until the omens are more favorable.

"Maybe the mathematics of the stars will be more lucky and more auspicious to us after we have talked again to the Four Witches of Kill."

Then Snakeknife and Warchariot called for singers, storytellers and readers of secret omens but the wise ones were reluctant to foretell bad outcomes and held back the fatal news until a better omen could be found.

CHAPTER FOUR
A PLOT FOR SEASPEAR

Then the woman calling herself the Queen of Justice asked for a huge amount of gold and silver and promised to examine stars and fortunes in a clear light of favorable omens.

Queen Snakeknife spoke to the king, Warchariot, "That sounds just what we need, someone to examine our fortunes in a favorable light rather than listen to these seers who hate us."

However, Warchariot was doubtful of the Queen of Justice but nevertheless agreed to hear her false omens in the hope that many would believe them to be true.

The Queen of Justice looked into a bowl of steaming water, then declared her vision. "I see the pale blue sky of victory. I see a haze of blue upon your hosts."

Then Snakeknife welcomed this vision of victory. "Now we can press ahead with the advice of the witches."

So Snakeknife made a hard and solemn promise, "I must try to win one of the enemy, one of the admirals of the Wavewarriors, to join with us and help us with our ships."

"But we have great heroes, too," cried Warchariot. "There is Sternrider who is swift and fearless. For he is generous in all his ways, whether in peace or with the sword or axe. His face is scarred with knife wounds and dart stabs. His vengeance is a storm of cut and killfury and yet his speech is fair and honorable, his judgments stand the test of time. His words can never be deflected from his purpose. His words are not stones, rather they are a cliff, a hill of rock rising out of the sea where the waves of change beat in on that strong island but that great rock remains immovable. His promises are kindly, strong and honest and they cannot be changed or weakened by spells of delusion woven by skilled witches.

"In times of battle, in a mighty host there are conflicts even within the mind, where each man doubts his cause yet fights like fury. There many warriors fight on to the death, although they may not know why they are fighting. Even here Sternrider leads them like a ship, a mighty ship of war cutting through waves.

"Where swords of red fight on to win or die, even here Sternrider rides a horse of iron to rout the vast battalions of the enemy and to cut thru even in a single combat. His one-on-one combats will open up a road of red like water pouring from a mighty rock. This tumbling waterfall that no one who is against him can withstand but rather they fall back in trembling fear.

"Sternrider tests the warriors on his side almost as much as those he fights against, so fearsome is his forward battle thrust. I would not like to be the Wavewarrior who stood against this lean, hard heart of stone. How have the tall tree trunks of fighting Seagulls been hewn down by this cold woodman of ice – Sternrider is our first war-wide fieldmarshal."

Snakeknife agreed, "Sternrider is our number one, yet I wish to hire also the number one of the Wavewarriors for his skill in boats – I mean, of course, the ship-wise sailor, Seaspear.

"Seaspear is a warrior of great skill – a sailor who manipulates the ships so that small craft can ring around and block the movements of great battle boats that carry sea warriors and their horses and their chariots. Seaspear can stand alone on a thin high prow where his men will steer the skiff thru any navy, even an army of strong fighting sailors, slaying the warriors to the left and right. Like a tornado he can cut thru fleets leaving a trail of drowning, floating bodies.

"I have heard reports of flotsam and destruction from the small boats of the warriors invading. Shields and spearshafts and clothes and belts and masks and helmets that float and bob like tiny boats. Scattered upon the waves like a huge shipwreck after Seaspear has driven thru their ranks, like a vi-king of all the sea invaders.

"He is a place of shelter for the poor, a refuge for the weak and miserable. He is a hill of safety for the rich . . to help them avoid the thieves and murderers. He is a vi-king, next to Waterbear, who overcomes the seas of seething turmoil. Also he is a prince whose word is law. This word and law must be obeyed by all, even himself, for his integrity is a spear of uprightness and swift reliability. In bravery, wisdom and knowledge, in fairness and in loyalty to his friends."

When Snakeknife had finished her eulogy of Seaspear, Warchariot spoke to her, "Then let Seaspear beware of you, Snakeknife,"

"Just so, Warchariot," the Snakeknife replied and laughed.

So Snakeknife and Warchariot pledged peace and respect for law to lure Seaspear to build up their ships and train their seamen in the skills of seacraft.

Warchariot spoke to Snakeknife, "It will not be easy to persuade a Wavewarrior to join us in the battle. Those Seagulls are the proud masters of the sea and they will never wish to split their ranks."

The Queen of Justice answered, "In that case you should vigorously deny to Seaspear and the other Wavewarriors that you have any intent to go to war."

And Snakeknife did so later when she met with Seaspear.

But in the Hillwolf camp, Queen Snakeknife stood up within her chariot and raised her javelin above her head as she rode all around her Hillwolf hosts, shouting, "Yes, war. Let us prepare for war."

***

Meanwhile, rumors of these plots and war ambitions drifted over the waves to the camp of the Wavewarriors and the fastness of the Waterbear.

Springvision pleaded with Seaspear not to join with Snakeknife and Warchariot – even though the Hillwolf king and queen had agreed that Seaspear was to be only a guide or guard to keep the peace as much as possible.

The swordswift warrior Summersailor, supreme fieldmarshal of the Wavewarriors, was the brother and vice-king of Waterbear. Summersailor and his sister Purplelake were in agreement that the task of Seaspear was to steer the many ships of peace between the Hillwolves and the Seagull sailors. So great was Seaspear as a warrior that few, if any, would dare to stand before him.

So Purplelake said, "Let Seaspear take the prow and lead the Hillwolves thru the straits of peace."

Seaspear did not believe in a coming war.

Seaspear sat with Waterbear upon the high roof of the Wavewarrior's palace on those great cliffs that overlooked the sea. There he spoke with Springvision and Gentleaf and the four fieldmarshals: the Summersailor, Whaleroarer, Icedragon and Stormleaper.

Suddenly the Mooncrow appeared there and perched on the rampart. "The King Warchariot and his Queen Snakeknife invite you, Seaspear, to a place of honor as admiral of all their fleet. You may remain as an advisor to King Waterbear – no secret of the Wolves will be kept from you."

Slowly the Mooncrow changed into a hag, withered and lean and warted. Limping around, she turned with a cunning sneer and flew away.

After the Mooncrow had flown away, Gentleaf spoke to Seaspear, "Do not accept or you will become our foe."

Springvision had the power of discernment in the gray realm of dreams, spirits and sleep. She pleaded with Seaspear, "Do not join the Wolves."

"I would be there only to guarantee the peace – reporting back to Waterbear," replied Seaspear.

"The great horsethief is Sternrider the Grim, for he controls the strategy of peace and all the diplomatic negotiations with me, as the best friend of Waterbear. Sternrider sees the peace as chariot-based – both sides defending and afraid to strike."

Then Summersailor and the other three fieldmarshals walked aside with Seaspear to discuss the offer made by King Warchariot regarding the leadership of all his ships.

Gentleleaf, the sister of Waterbear and the Queen of his close friend Seaspear, pleaded with her brother, the king, for Seaspear not to take up the position of admiral of the fleet for Warchariot. She pleaded that she feared a darker side would soon emerge and no clear peace would come. "I do not trust Snakeknife or the Warchariot. I would not turn my back on them, my brother."

Waterbear agreed, "You still will have the help of our own fleet to come and go and maybe we can steer a path of peace between our peoples. We have still the best warheroes in our ranks – the four fieldmarshals for our four fronts of battle – the seas, the hills, the plains, the sky: Stormleaper, Whaleroarer, Icedragon and the Summersailor. We can still show with pride the emblems and flags of war: Crias, Crows, Buzzards and Seahawks."

Springvision spoke to her close friend Gentleleaf. "Sternrider needs Seaspear to guide his fleet. But I do not agree that we can trust King Warchariot, the master of Sternrider. Sternrider is a fieldmarshal of honor, respected and well-loved by all his fighters. Warchariot is a cunning king who rules by fear."

And Gentleleaf replied, "I will speak to Seaspear. Sternrider tried to use the gallant Bay to steal the horses of the brave White stallion but Oceanhorse was sharp and vigilant and plunged away to follow Foresthorse and to retrieve the horses of the East. Sternrider's not only their fieldmarshal but also their negotiator – the only effective leader of their warriors."

Then the Wavewarriors drank, from the clear goblets, the water from the bright and pleasant hillside. Then they sat and ate the venison of speed and elegance and sword dexterity.

"I want to have a foot in both our camps," said Seaspear.

"Let us agree, Seaspear," said brave Waterbear, "that we, the two great warriors of the world, will never take the field against each other. I will trust you to keep the peace between our two great lands and I will trust you always to give us whatever information we need to keep the peace, even though you will be the admiral of the Wolves ships."

"This I agree," said Seaspear. And they shook hands as a pledge based on their longtime friendship.

Waterbear and Seaspear were both agreed on the grounds that they had no war plans to hide.

Seaspear addressed brave Waterbear and the others. "Of course, there is a difference with Warchariot over the split kingdom of the world but East has lived with

West over the decades and we can dwell in mutual respect, trading and intermingling for longer still."

So King Waterbear agreed with vi-king Seaspear, telling him. "But Seaspear, as the admiral of both fleets, be ever wary and watchful, day and night."

But Gentleleaf did not agree, "I do not fear a threat that comes out in the night behind your back but rather I fear an onslaught on your mind due to the cunning of their witchcraft."

Gentleleaf begged her husband, "Be aware Seaspear and know that Warchariot and the Snakeknife are not to be trusted to walk the paths of peace. They plan and plot for war to conquer the world."

"I know this, Gentleleaf, I have heard these rumors – the stuff of ladies gossip but that is why I need to be their confidant and ally so that the Seagulls will be well prepared for any information I can bring them. Our Seagull sailors do not need an admiral other than Waterbear. They are well armed and skilled. Their ships are fit and clean and ready for war."

"You will learn nothing if they do not plan to make a sea invasion – rather the rumors suggest a plot to make a war by land," said Gentleleaf.

Seaspear spoke up, "Then that will not involve me, Gentleleaf."

"Snakeknife and Warchariot are newly the King and Queen but they are inexperienced, so they delegate the day-to-day war tactics to Sternrider the Grim and Admiral Seaspear," said King Waterbear.

But Gentleleaf was puzzled to see why Seaspear should go to work for the Hillwolves.

And Gentleleaf spoke privately to Waterbear about this.

"Seaspear has said that we are not at war. I know he works to keep the peace. He knows that there will always be squabbles over who owns what. But now I fear he will have divided loyalties."

Then Gentleleaf later spoke quietly to her husband Seaspear about war.

"My sister Springvision is the queen of all the Seagulls. She is married to King Waterbear. We are both worried that you plan to leave us and go to work for Snakeknife and Warchariot."

But Seaspear disagreed, "I have already made it clear that I do not work for them. I go to work only for the fieldmarshal, Sternrider the Grim, a man of great integrity. I go as admiral to help him trim his ships. It is true that Sternrider takes his orders from Snakeknife and Warchariot but I have their permission to tell you all I know and you can pass that on to Waterbear. This is the proof surely that Warchariot is peaceful and that he and Snakeknife and their fieldmarshal Sternrider have no desire for war against the Seagulls."

"Perhaps. But I still fear their machinations. Please do not trust them. Stay with the Wavewarriors," pleaded Gentleleaf.

"Dear Gentleleaf, I will be out at sea doing my sailing as usual with the ships and Waterbear has said that he agrees but to be watchful. And so I will be wary and watchful at all times. I will return home often and join you here beloved Gentleleaf."

But Gentleleaf remained sad with a foreboding. It was as though a cloud had blocked the sunlight that once had shone on the garden of her marriage.

***

Later, in the camp of the Hillwolves, Sternrider presided over a council of peace with Winterwarrior, Warchariot and the Snakeknife to welcome Seaspear as an admiral. "Next to the Waterbear, the Seaspear is the greatest warrior and shipman of the Seagulls. We have the right-hand man, they have what's left. Surely this is an omen of success. Let us drink wine to Seaspear. Soon our ships will be as taut and tight, well-roped and armed as any in the world."

Seaspear raised a glass of the red wine of courage, "May both our peoples live and work in peace."

CHAPTER FIVE
SPRINGVISION

Sternrider welcomed Seaspear to the Castle of Snakeknife and Warchariot. They went to the throne room where there were four high chairs for talking and consultations. The king and queen smiled and shook hands with Seaspear.

Sternrider bowed with elegance and stated, "We need a man of the sea to help our sailors. A skilled and masterly vi-king, like you, Seaspear.

"While we try hard to avoid a clash between the Hillwolves and the Seagull Wavewarriors, we still will need to know and like each other. Your coming here to help us with our fleet will prove we have no hidden secret plans. Also, we know of your great combat warriors, the swiftest and most deadly in the world: the Whaleroarer, Stormleaper, Icedragon and Summersailor.

"But who is the boy Wallwave who is training and what is the strange story of his birth? Is it true that he is one of the Immortals?"

Seaspear replied, "I will tell you his whole story – he is mortal but his godfather is Truthteller the Immortal with the silver darts of truth. Truthteller wears the white cloak of invisibility."

Then Seaspear sat beside the thrones and stared into the distant visions of a dream.

"The boy Wallwave, eldest son of Waterbear, is now hard training in the arts of combat with his great-uncle the old Shadowhero. There he is schooled in javelin and sword, dagger and spear-throwing, shield defense. He lives, of course, in fosterage with a family who are well skilled in war and fish and sea.

"Wallwave is skilled in all. He will be ready to stand alone in combat and in war in about three or four years. He will be well experienced and matured in five years' time."

Then Snakeknife bowed solemnly and addressed the Warchariot. Giving a sly, sideways glance, she murmured, "The boy Wallwave will be fit for deadly warfare and trained and combat ready in about four years?"

Seaspear was still entranced in a faraway dream and continued the story, "The boy Wallwave had a strange origin. Ten years ago Waterbear opened his castle that stood beside a harbor of the ocean for a three day festival of the sea where the Wavewarriors tested their skills of fishing, hunting and warfare. There they recounted boasts of their past combats, displayed mock battles, sham fights and tricks of fighting. There they caught fish and roasted them on spits while they sat by and bragged of their war exploits. Then they took out their hunting dogs to chase and round up, find and fetch small game and birds. The leader of the dog pack was Guardhunt – a fine and loyal and good-natured dog – whom all the other dogs feared and respected for his great strength and speed and sense of smell.

"On the third day they rode into the hills to hunt for deer. The dogs were led by Guardhunt who was the hound of Whaleroarer the hero. A beautiful roe rose up before the hunters as Guardhunt, with a pack of dogs, rushed forward and began to frolic and fawn around the roe.

"The warriors were astounded to see that Guardhunt made no attempt to kill or cower the roe but rather made a friend of it. The other dogs took their cue from the pack leader and loped around and bowed and licked in fun. The roe turned sharply from the beaten track and headed for the castle of Waterbear – followed by the baying, playful Guardhunt. The dogs escorted the roe into the castle – all closely followed by the Seagull warriors.

"The hunting troop continued their pursuit of other game as Waterbear remarked to Whaleroarer, "I cannot understand why Guardhunt was so friendly and protective. However, the roe will still be there inside the castle keep when we get back.

"The Wavewarriors continued on the hunt and later, at the end of the day, they returned home with salmon and wild boar for their festival. When they sat down to feast at the open fire in the courtyard of the castle of Waterbear, there was no sign of any roe or deer. They sang the songs of old and told their stories and drank their toasts of wine to their sea heroes.

"Late in the evening Waterbear walked across the courtyard to the well and the bright fountain that sprang out of the ground – a waterspring of the sun that glittered and gleamed in the pale moonlight. There stood a women, young and beautiful, whom he had never seen before. He asked her, 'Who are you?'

"She replied, 'I am the roe that Guardhunt and the pack escorted here earlier in the day. Where is Guardhunt?'

"And Waterbear replied to the strange young girl, 'No doubt he is over in the Whaleroarer camp, whose dog he is. But why have you come here?'

"As the young girl answered him, Waterbear saw that her hair was black and thick and loose for washing. She held in her hands a gold and silver comb with a silver basin decorated with bluebirds and colored gems set all around the rim. Her skin was yellow golden like the dawn. The moonlight shone upon her yellow shoulders above a bodice of blue silk as she prepared to wash her hair in the silver bowl. Her long white skirt was laced with golden fringes and blue-gold brooches shone at her silken neck. Her eyes were brown as the sunflower in the summer – a brown bulb surrounded by bright yellow leaves when the bees fly round and buzz in the hazy air. Her lips were as red as rowanberries in springtime and her teeth as white as the bright foam of the wave. The yellow light of the moon was on her face as her dark eyebrows rose like thin black arches. Her voice was like soft bells of waterfalls in a cave of tinkling waters and rainbows.

"Her step was full of grace and elegance, even and balanced and like a dancing queen. Around her was an aura of flowers and trees – a faint aroma of blue days in woodlands. All ladies of high birth are beautiful until you see the beauty of Springvision. It is as though she sprang out of a sea of tropical green grasses and brown corals shining and shimmering in a pool of sunlight.

" 'I am Springvision, a princess of the orient,' she told Waterbear. 'The old witch Meteoreyes once envied me my youth. She asked me to enter a trance where she would invade my mind and memory. She planned to take me over to possess and to hold my spirit and my mind, to use my youth to ensnare young kings and princes. When I refused her promises of paradise, the Four Witches of Kill gathered around. Meteoreyes put a long spell on me and changed me into the roe that Guardhunt guided here to-day. The spell worked well for everywhere, except the royal sovereign. For it was not permitted by the Powers of Good for the witches to take over the kingdoms of the world. So I took flight and fled the woods and hills to find this fastness.'

" 'You are a vision beside a spring of beauty so I will call you now and ever Springvision,' Waterbear told her.

"All around them shone a purple aura covering well and spring. Wild boar, salmon, cups and plates were laid beside the water from the hillside fountain.

"A tall thin grey-haired man appeared dressed in the plain clothes of a wandering student. He addressed the two – Waterbear and Springvision – 'Eat and drink here, within this pure purple aura. This water comes from a bright and pleasant hillside.'

"Springvision was thirsty and she drank long and deep with a large helping from the silver salmon. Waterbear ate just a little salmon and a large piece of boar, drinking it down with many cups of hillside fountain water.

"All the food and drink gleamed in the purple glow but after they had eaten, the aura died and the food and water returned to its former color.

"The grey-haired man said, 'I am Truthteller and I have enchanted all this food and water to celebrate your coming marriage and the sons who will come after. I will guide your lives but only as you have eaten of this food and drunk the water in the purple glow. It was your choice. That was the boar of courage, of speed and strength in battle. That was the salmon of wisdom and the water was the crystal stream of truth and honor.'

" 'If only we had known this,' cried Waterbear.

"And Truthteller replied, in his keen wisdom, 'We cannot all have courage, skill and honor in equal measures. Such is the wheel of fortune – it must spin uniquely for each person. Only your eldest son, the Wallwave, will have all the attributes of a great hero. He will show courage, skill and honor in battle.'

"Then Truthteller stepped into the fountain spring and disappeared from the eyes of the young couple.

"Later, Waterbear and Springvision were married and lived in their castle, keep and outer courtyard. For seven years Springvision did not leave in case the spell of metamorphoses from the four witches should again transform her. During this time Waterbear stood beside her to protect her from spells and potions of the envious witch.

"At the end of seven years, Hillwolves sailing in small, scrappy boats as cutthroat pirates, invaded the islands of the Wavewarriors and plundered and pillaged all the Seagull people. Waterbear then had to leave his Seagull castle and gathered together his warriors and ships to fall upon the sea robbers and the thieves. He bade a tender farewell to the Queen Springvision and warned her never to leave the palace walls. She promised never to leave the castle keep or courtyard until he had returned with all his heroes after they had thrown the pirates into the sea. He feared that the dread spell of Meteoreyes would seize Springvision and change her once again into a roe.

"Waterbear then sailed away and as Springvision waved from the fastness wall he cried out and reminded her, 'Take care; do not step outside our own castle courtyard; do not speak to a stranger; keep our faith and soon I will come back; then once again we will be happy.'

"Waterbear pushed hard against the pirates, wrecked and burnt their ships but the sea-thieves fought hard and every inch of ocean foam was bought with Seagull blood.

"At last the pirates were left dying and dead, floating with scraps of wood and ropes and sails, choking and crying out in the green seaweed.

"Then Waterbear and his Wavewarriors sailed back, his hands still dripping wet with the red blood of bitter combats and piraticide.

"As they sailed North and East to their homeland, Waterbear thought only of his coming home and of the warm reunion with Springvision.

"As the sharp ship of brave Waterbear cut through the waves approaching the Wavewarrior's castle, shining in sunlight and looking over the sea, the Waterbear could see no glimpse or glimmer, no skirt or shawl, no handwaving or scarf flying high in the sky to welcome him back home. Nor was there any face in any window. And when the longboat of the Waterbear sailed into his wide harbor, all the servants avoided his firm gaze and looked away in solemn silence and uneasy quietness as though they were glancing sideways at the king.

"Brave Waterbear shivered and felt a lump, a stone, sinking far down inside his stomach. 'Where is the Queen, Springvision? Why does she not come to meet me here?' asked Waterbear.

"An older servant turned to Waterbear and looked him in the eye, 'The Queen Springvision is gone, brave Waterbear. One day a figure that looked like you appeared outside the courtyard with a great dog that looked like our old Guardhunt with other dogs and a chariot nearby. We saw a shade, a shape that looked like Waterbear cry out in pain as though he had been stabbed. He walked like one who had been wounded, limped slowly towards the gate, then shouted out, 'Please help us Springvision, we are wounded. Guardhunt and I have suffered in the war. I need to catch my breath. Help me, my Queen!'

" 'We urged Springvision not to go. We pleaded that we should be allowed to help him, for we suspected that it was a sameshape conjured from the pit of image manipulation. But Springvision ran to help the darkling figure outside the gates. As she came close to it she saw the vague shape shimmer in the sun and realized it was not Waterbear; the dog was not Guardhunt. It snarled and growled. She screamed and shrank back but it was too late; the hideous witch, old Meteoreyes, struck out and changed Springvision into a red roe. The dog, false Guardhunt, threw himself upon her and as a roe she fled into the woods.

" 'Of course, we seized our weapons and pursued the roe and the old haggard

Meteoreyes, following the sounds of horses and barking of dogs but they were gone and lost among the bushery.

" 'Springvision had been so quick in dashing out that she had metamorphized in a minute and disappeared from sight in a few seconds. Then we could see neither Queen Springvision, nor dog, nor pack, nor roe, nor loathsome witch. We have felt guilt and terror ever since.'

"Waterbear said, 'Feel neither guilt nor terror for it is my responsibility to find her and break the spell and set her free and bring her home.'

"Then the Waterbear went to visit Whitehair, the niece of Summersailor. Only a child, she had the gift of foresight and discernment of spirits. Young Whitehair told the king, 'When the seas recoil and whip into high waves, go to the oceanside and call aloud to Springvision. Then winds will roar and carry abroad your call and when she hears, your Queen will do the rest.'

"So Waterbear went back to his own room above the sea and waited for the storm. For three days and three nights he did not eat but prayed to the powers of good in the universe. Then, on a nearby island the earth shook and lava poured out from the fiery hilltop as waves leapt up and clawed in the fierce wind. Realizing that the four elements were in harmony in a deep and ominous and auspicious way, Waterbear took his hawk and hounds and sailed on the rough seas among the little islands and called, 'Springvision! We have come to find you.' "

After telling the story of Springvision, Seaspear awoke from his long storytrance.

CHAPTER SIX

THE BOY WALLWAVE

But Snakeknife still persisted, "Tell us more of the boy Wallwave as a fighting force."

Then Seaspear lapsed again into a storytrance and told the king and queen how the boy Wallwave was growing up as a tall warrior.

"The moon began to fade in the dawn light and soon the sun arose upon the red ocean, sending its rays along the choppy waves.

"The real Guardhunt leapt up and whined and moaned and barked as he left the boat and swam to a small island. Waterbear steered his small ship after Guardhunt and there he found Springvision in a pool of corals, flowers and leaves. Swimming beside her was the boy Wallwave floating among the lilies.

"The deep wallwave of the seas recoiling, the earth turmoiling, lava and flames arising and the loud roar of thunder cracking the island had smashed apart the spell of the four witches and set Springvision free to return home. Waterbear acclaimed the stormchild as his son and named the boy Wallwave as the future king.

"The Wallwave was yellow-skinned and oriental with dark hair and brown eyes like sunflowers set in a gold ring of yellow leaves just like his mother, Springvision. He was strong and active in the pools and waves. Even at an early age of one or two he broke the weapons that young children play with and at three years he begged from Waterbear the weapons of a fully grown warrior to play with. When attacked by a black wolf at four, he speared the wolf to death. At five he strangled a young bear that had attacked him. Later in that year he stabbed a shark to death under the water. If he can do these things at five, what will he be able to do in battle when he is fully grown?

"Then he was sent to foster with a farming family who fished and sailed and fought as foot soldiers. Their name is Kim and they love Wallwave dearly. His great-uncle Shadowhero – an old man now retired from active war - trains him in all the feats of combat and hard fighting.

"Before he went to train with the Shadowhero, he won the magic Shield of Roar that warns of danger. This shield was presented to him by the popular acclaim of Seagull heroes, sitting in council on the rules of warfare. Its orle fringe quivers when it hears the sound of coming danger and lets out a roar of warning to its owner. The young boy Wallwave also won the prize of the Bonespear that thirsts for blood and never fails to crunch bone. Also, the Rainbow-Hardblade sword that paints a rainbow in the sky when it is whirled high in the air by any warrior. This also was a prize won by the Wallwave.

"He is well armed with all the accoutrements of war and works hard to perform his hero feats of sword and shield and spear for Shadowhero."

Seaspear awoke from his storytrance that told of the growing up of the boy Wallwave. Then he took his leave of the

Warchariot and Snakeknife and left with Sternrider and went with him to talk of warrior ships.

When Snakeknife and Warchariot were alone and out of hearing they lowered their voices and made plans for war.

Snakeknife then turned and sneered to Warchariot, "The Four Witches of Kill have served us well for they have eaten the squirming, slippery eels of sly and cunning. They have drunken also the red wine of delusion and dark vision. Soon the chief heroes of the Wavewarriors will be enchanted by the flowers and perfumes concocted by the witches.

"Soon their four great fieldmarshals: Stormleaper, Whaleroarer, Icedragon and the Summersailor will drift into sloth and dreams, though they have eaten well of the salmon of wisdom and the wild boar of courage. They will drink the water of honor and truth from the cool fountain that flows on a bright and pleasant hillside in the sun. Yet, soon they will fall and blunder all around among the blooms in the steaming purple jungles of mindmadness and image manipulation.

"The Four Witches of Kill are sly and sleekit. They have given a five-point exercise, simple enough for any child to play on its five fingers or on its five toes. *One* – enchant the four chief heroes of the Seagulls to weaken them and drive them far away. *Two* – hire a false seer to stir up our Hillwolves. What does it matter if she lies or not – many will die in any case. At least they can be lifted up in hope, before they die in sudden cold despair. *Three* – hire top men from the Seagull's fleet to further weaken them and strengthen us. *Four* – find a hostage to constrain the foe. I cannot see who that might be, at present. But, no doubt, we will find one in due course. *Five* – steal horses to unmount their chariots, which soon will lie in ruins, rot and rust. Then we will drive thru and civilize their land, dividing it more fairly among ourselves. That is our plan and we are well ahead in all the paths that lead to victory. We have at least three years before the advent of Wallwave, upon whom spells will never work. This is the case also with Waterbear. Father and son enjoy the same immunity and will be fit to throw their long cold waves against us."

So Warchariot and Snakeknife came to see that they had only three years to wage a war and pressed ahead with all their plans and plots.

***

So, at this time, the boy Wallwave trained with Shadowhero and the foster family.

Springvision also visited at times to teach the future king of right and wrong. "For these moral judgments," she said, "were equally important as feats of combat and sharp self-defense.

"There are two forces in the universe, forces of right and wrong. Both kinds of spirit are almost everywhere, except around the thrones of sovereign kings who have become obsessed with either right or wrong. These spirits make or break all the plans and purposes of men and women. Spirits of good are there to help you build, develop or create. Spirits of ill are there to help destroyers of the things you are building.

"Life is make or break – every act you do and every thought you think will fly out into the universe of spirit. There it will reach its zenith when it hits the wall of the universe. There it is doubled. Our White horse is the symbol of good powers. The Bay horse of the West is the symbol of ill to help others destroy the things you build.

"Likewise, all the acts of crude destruction will be multiplied and sent straight back to you along the spirit paths of thought and sleep – sometimes also known as the Powers of Win for they are so determined to win at all costs. They will destroy and kill and steal just to come out on top and gain the victory at any price. You need to know that all your skills and feats are solely to defend the right and honor for that is the only purpose of a king."

So the young Wallwave trained in skills and courage and in the honor that befits a king.

But at this time, the Four Witches of Kill brewed up strange visions in their fiery lair – visions that they controlled with odors and perfumes. These weird illusions from the other world were given form and substance by the potions of the four witches. These ghosts were made alive to act in the world of man and so lead men astray into the mists of ocean. Such would be the fate of all the fieldmarshals of the Wavewarriors, together with their foremost battle champions.

Then these brave heroes and their chief combatants would leave the East, its islands and real seas, to stray into the flowers, plants and jungles of the illusionary Isles of the Everyoung. Thus all the islands of the Wavewarriors and all the eastern side of the globe itself would lie at the mercy of Warchariot and Snakeknife's cruel grasp of tax and kill.

For what can one man do, even Waterbear, against a skilled well-trained and seething army?

***

Queen Snakeknife called out loudly from her throne, "Send for the woman known as Queen of Justice."

Warchariot shook his head but sat in silence. The Queen of Justice entered and bowed low.

Snakeknife dismissed all servants from the hall. "I want your prophecy for all my army," she told the Queen of Justice.

The Queen of Justice answered her. "In case my prophecy should not be favorable and people then be too upset to pay me, for I am interested only in truth, I always ask for my small gold piece fee before I read the signs and constellations."

Then Snakeknife handed her a purse of gold and asked, "Is this enough?"

"It is a privilege," replied the false seer.

"Tell no one of this," said the queen.

"Of course not, Queen Snakeknife," replied the seer, who then went outside and cleared a space to light a fire of twigs, capturing on a leaf a weak pattern of smoke. Holding the leaf up to the light and scrutinizing it, she mumbled and muttered unintelligibly then cried in a loud voice, "I see a battle – Hillwolves are fighting the Wavewarriors. I cannot see clearly if this is just a skirmish or a small part of a much wider war but I can see the Hillwolves win the day and the Wavewarriors are destroyed to the last man. I see Hillwolves plundering the Seagull ships of gold and weapons and accoutrements and all the spoils of war. I hear the wails of the Seagull's wives and children now enslaved. It is too terrible to watch."

The seer threw the smoke-stained leaf away and left.

Snakeknife was pleased but Warchariot kept silent as word of the false omens spread around.

CHAPTER SEVEN
A MESSENGER ON HORSEBACK

Windweasel muttered to the other Witches of Kill, "Little by little the way the tiny cat ate the big fish let us persevere and scatter their warriors and champions."

One day the Stormleaper saddled his hunting horse, a white horse like the great stallion Oceanhorse and rode out in the field to look for deer. Instead, he saw a young girl dressed in the armor and highboots of a warriorqueen riding a royal steed from out of the West. She wore a golden crown and a silk cloak of purple decked with dazzling silvery stars. Her skin was whiter than the swan on water. Her lips were softer than red wine mixed with honey. Her eyes were like the clear blue skies of summer. Two gold hoops hung from both her ears. Her hair was the same color as the hoops and flowed in thick locks over her shoulder. Her pink cheeks were like two peaches in the bloom of Fall.

The warriorqueen pulled up her horse - a bay almost as big as the Great Bay of the West. Her steed was shod with silver and was harnessed in red bronze and in brown leather with golden smallbells tinkling as she rode along. She firmly held a bridle with a gold bit and sat upon a saddle worked in copper. Her horse was cloaked to shield him from the cold in a purple woven tunic of pure wool. His mane was gray and flowing in the wind as he shook his head and bowed in pride and friendship.

Stormleaper asked the queen, "Where do you come from?"

She answered him, "My father is the king of the Isle of the Everyoung. I had a vision that showed you to me in your war accoutrements, sword and shield and copper coat of mail, your horseman's boots and wrist enstrengthens, your chainbelt ringed around with dirks and daggers – also your horned helmet, ready for combat. The vision said your name is the Stormleaper. I need a warrior like you beside my throne. Come with me to the Isles of the Everyoung and bring your warriors with you for company and also for security, for we are attacked everyday by enemies who try to steal our land and all its peace."

"But tell me who you are, besides a warriorqueen?" Stormleaper asked. "I see that you are beautiful but so are many – that is not enough for me to marry you and go with you."

The queen replied, "Then come and join me in the Isles of the Everyoung. You are free to leave at any time. And you will be protected by all your heroes. No one will entrap you. Take a small sip of red wine and if you find it good to drink, quaff the whole bottle. For you will find that I have many gifts. Besides the gift of beauty, I have the gift of voice and singing, the gift of purity, the gift of handiwork and skillful hands, the gift of wisdom and witty conversation. My name is Tear for sadness and for joy. Your day will not be dull. It will be sunny."

Then the Stormleaper laughed and told the queen, "I would not go with you unless you were able to keep above the talk of heroes but what is this far island of the sea where everything is young and lives forever?

Would I be happy there? I am mature, a battle-hardened warrior of many wars."

"I say, drink some and judge it for yourself. There is red wine and drinking horns of mead and fruits all the year round, flowers of strong smells."

Tear plucked a blue flower from her cloak of silk and threw it at Stormleaper. He caught it and breathed it. Soon a vision rose around him of blues and reds and coral plants and rocks and streaming trees and birds of many colors.

Then Tear continued, "In those isles the branches bend with pears and apples, leaves and yellow blossoms. For in that land of fruit and nuts and herbs, there no one dies and no one ebbs away. Time is not there to waste away your life. The day of harvest is at hand all year with feasts and rich gifts of silver, gold and gems and music of mind-relaxing melodies. There are also swords swift enough and sharp enough for any cloaks of fine silk and horses fit for combat, black and tan hounds and falcons for the hunt.

"My father's royal helmet in the battle will save you from the thrust of dirk and spear or from the cleaving swing of the wild axe. Also, I will give you a sword within its sheath that when it is once unsheathed has never yet failed to strike out a fatal blow. No one has ever escaped alive from that sharp sword – so light and keenly balanced is that weapon.

"You will have shirts of blue satin, coats of mail and armor. There will be tenderest calves fed only on nuts and herbs for you and all your strong vi-kings to feast on. Jewels of many colors – red and purple, all will be yours. And many serving girls, each with a voice more gentle than a bird to sing in a sweet chorus of dream music. Many strong warriors skilled in battle contests to toss high in the air their feats of combat, challenging you and your men in war-display of keen sham-fights of dangerous false battles.

"There you will get beauty, skill and power. You will learn of wonders from the land of spirit. In those far isles miracles take place on the strange landscape that stretches from one mind and imagination to meet with others in the dead of night. There will be colors and shapes and smells of mind illusions and I myself will be there as your queen."

The voice of Tear was so melodious, her beauty was so mind-stunning and brilliant, that Stormleaper heard her words like one under a spell of silence. When she spoke, no bee buzzed in the flowers, no bird sang, no stream or river gurgled, no breeze rustled among the trees. A silence fell on all until she stopped speaking and the spell ended.

Stormleaper rode his white horse behind Tear, following her with all his warrior heroes, until they reached the long sands of the sea. They galloped over high dunes of straggling grass, over the wet shore where tides had licked, over the wave crests sweeping out to the ocean, over the green seaweeded hills of turmoil into the slip and slide of heaving water.

They traveled like wind over the salt-sea smiling mountains of foam – followed by great seabirds flying in squadrons that cried aloud like crias, to warn the heroes who were following Tear. Through the rainbows and bright sunbeams they rode on through beaches lit by pearls and silvery fish, over the cities of the sea with pinnacle, towers

and turrets and peaks of minarets –
gleaming and flittering in the bright
moonlight. Beside the flowers and green
grass and the seashells, the marbles and the
silver statuettes. Cities that seemed to fade
and disappear from sight before a second
glance was possible.

Far in the sky a vision arose before
them, a huge and panoramic view of war –
the witch Windweasel, old, shriveled and
wrinkled, leering in withered, toothless,
cruel laughter. Her claws and skinny arms
held closely to the reins and bridle of the
Great Bay horse just like the stallion ridden
by Queen Tear.

There, opposite the Bay, a Seagull
warrior, wearing a purple cloak, pointed a
spear at the old hag. There also an oriental
warrior, mounted on the Great White
Stallion Oceanhorse. He was fully armored
in all the accoutrements of combat. Above
the two great horses flew the Mooncrow,
circling above them with the caws of war.

It was not clear to Stormleaper and his
men what this strange vision meant but it
soon faded.

And Tear told them, "This is a sky picture of war. War is the last thing that you want or need." And Tear assured them that the tapestry in the air meant nothing but that a great war was coming soon. Then, sure enough, the sky was darkening into the grayish mists of cloud. Then vision all around grew dim and shivery and the presence of Windweasel seemed more real as rain, lightning and thunders fell upon them and froze them to the bone. Daggers of rain, javelins of lightning stabbed them through and through.

They fled before the wind like leaves of fall and their brave horses chomped and pranced in terror through woods and weeds and bushes and shrubberies. They were well soaked and saturated with the storm and well entangled around them were the flowers, grasses and herbs of that great turbulence.

At last they left the blustery gale behind them and rode more gently into the warm Isles of the Everyoung – a land of sun and healing. As they dismounted at the happy river, the smell of afterstorm was strong upon them as they breathed deeply in relief to be there. The isle where they now stood was like a gem set in the surround of a silvery strand for all the shores were white with ocean pebbles.

The people of the Isles of the Everyoung were laughing and relaxed and welcoming. They waved their hands to Tear and the Stormleaper. They came and went to caves in a white hillside. These caves were dry and overlooked the river and flowers and bushes and rich blossoming trees of heavy blooms and humming, homing bees. Red, blue and green and yellow birds sang out and jumped and pecked in the green clover fields. The Everyoung were just as cheerful as those many-colored birds that ran and flew among the sunny branches of the forests. There, where the giant weeping willows wore green cloaks of shadeful leaves as shields from the hot sun.

Queen Tear dismounted and welcomed Stormleaper, bowing to all his champions, "Be happy, for here there is no sorrow and no death; there is no sickness, no wasting away on the torture rack of age where bones grow old and bodies shrivel up in pain and cancer. Here there is no gangrene in the bone, no blockage in the blood. There is no weakness in veins or arteries, rather the body breathes in full fresh air and functions like an athlete.

"In war, in combat or in love or dancing, here it is always summer. Land and sea and rivers are always warm and soothing to the mind. Here you may eat of many fruits and meats, honeys and fish or drink the wine of grapes. Whatever you desire, it shall be yours."

And Stormleaper took Tear to be his queen and all his champions also took companions. There they lived in a haze of warm sunlight, They exercised with swords and spears and shields and all the tricks and feats of martial arts, with tossing and somersaulting in the air to match any foe in speed and combat skill. Here they lived, forgetting their old haunts in the cold and icy valleys of the East, forgetting the old horseback haunts in snow, the ale-feasts, round the fire in wintertime, the conquest of the cruel grasping enemy and all the things of home in the real world.

Stormleaper did not long for the old ways for he was happy there with lovely Tear. But sometimes in the night he saw, in dreams, the things of old, the hunting of the deer, the chase for the wild boar, the falcon set to round up the wild game, fishing the icy lakes and cold waterfalls and rushing rapids.

Then Stormleaper would rise out of his dreams and walk the warm paths of beauty in the night.

CHAPTER EIGHT
A CALL FROM A CURRAGH

Whaleroarer was the great fieldmarshal whose warriors fought for the high ground in any dispute of war. His was the battalion that fought hill battles and captured the waterfalls and rocky rapids. So they were known as crows – their battle banner was a black crow with a yellow beak. But winning hard-fought battles of the mountains was never easy. Sometimes men were captured and taken far away to distant islands.

And so Whaleroarer set his mind to search the distant islands of the West to find some of these captives. "We are now at peace – at least as much as we will ever be – for there are always horsethieves and the like. So let us build a curragh for high seas that will be large enough to rescue men."

The curragh was built with forty oxen hides, all hard brown leather, soaked in juice of bark. She was fitted out with oars and masts and painted with pitch to make her watertight. She had great sails of heavy linen with ropes and hooks for catching shark and other harvests of the sea. The boat was given waterskins, chickens laying eggs, other foods and was filled with many kegs of wine and ale. Her hold was packed with all the accoutrements of war - fierce screaming swords and vigorous battleaxes, long spears and slender javelins and daggers, shields and horned helmets to protect from thrusts made by the enemy. All the best champions of the high ground battalions of the Seagulls were proud to take their places in this craft.

When everything was fitted and shipshape, Whaleroarer cried out, "Let the gods of mountains take over our safe journeying and return with many men now missing from our ranks. Men in captivity or slavery, who will be glad to rejoin our other warships."

They pulled hard on their oars and swept the curragh out to the open sea where waves like mountains rolled and moved sideways trying to avoid them.

"Stand still, wild waves," Whaleroarer cried. But they ignored him with contempt and rolled the more.

The heroes laughed at Whaleroarer's dismay and told him, "We are alone on this great ocean – there is no discipline here. No giving of orders to sea creatures of the deep."

The great hills of green seaweeded mountains leapt like a forest of wild wood all around them. At last they saw there was no land or island on any part of the steep waves that leapt high above them. But rather there was only an unbroken round horizon that stretched in a circle about them. It was like a circus ring with sharks and whales leaping instead of horses. White-bellied salmon ranged like circus dogs and up above them bluebirds flew like gymnasts. Dolphins and black staring seals popped their curious heads to look around amazed out of the waves to see what they could see. Just like the appreciative audiences who gape in wonderment at chariot-horses in a real circus.

They rowed on and on and looked astonished at these circus freaks flying in fun and swimming in display until they saw an island on the round horizon. The coast was golden sand where the curragh landed. They camped out on the shore and drank their ale and lit their fires and cooked their pork and chicken. They ate their fish and fruit and slept till sunrise.

Then Whaleroarer arose in the cold dawn and, wearing his accoutrements of war, strode like a fighting cock around the island looking for enemies but none were there. But many crows flew out of all the trees and cawed and cried and croaked at Whaleroarer as though to warn him of impending danger.

Whaleroarer and his men were sailing around the island on the day that followed when a large ship was seen on the horizon. It was a long high craft of shining white with a carved crow upon the prow. This was the symbol of Whaleroarer's war battalion that fought upon the high hills and rapids.

When the round boat sailed close to the white ship they could not see a crew or any sailors inside the ship, except a beautiful red woman with red eyes and bright red hair. Her crimson hair hung loosely over her shoulders and blew back in the breeze. Her eyebrows were as black as crow. Her eyes were like large rubies set in a blue-gray sky. Her long strong fingers were like red knives but tipped with sharp black dirks. She stood proudly aloft in the ship's prow as splashes of foam and wind blew fiercely around her.

The great sail on her ship that drove it forward was also emblazoned with a large black crow – the symbol of the hills and waterfalls division of the Seagull army. For the crow flies up to perch on the pinnacles of springs and rapids.

Her tunic, with long silk skirt and sleeves, was blue and pressed back by the wind and ocean spray. Calm dignity and strength were in her voice as she raised up one hand and pointed at Whaleroarer, "Come with me. I am Sigh. Bring all your heroes. I am come from the Isles of the Everyoung, the Isle of Waterfalls and Rainbows.

"There Death does not visit. Our feasts last for ever. There we live quietly and do kind things without the quarrels and the wars of earth. There is no envy and no destruction. There all is Make, nothing is ever Break. No pain or cancer withers up your body. There you will always walk upon two legs. There you will never walk upon one leg or three, with crutch or cane or walking stick, or none, or never be wheeled around by younger servants.

"There you will never enter the torture chamber of old age with the keen and ruthless torturers, Gangrene and Cripple, Heart Attack and Stroke, Tumor and Poison, Cancer and Wasteaway. Those cruel cold mechanics of the blood and bone – they dash around attentively and turn the wheels and stretch the racks and pull the levers in this grim gymnasium. Avoid that place called Old Age – it is torment – unfit for any lithe and healthy hero.

"There is another country you should seek – the country that delights the mind of all who join with me. Come join the dreamscape isles, the isle of hills and waterfalls and fountains where rainbows play and dance among the rapids, where the proud crow flies to the pinnacle of the high rocks.

"I have the gifts of sovereign rule that I will pass to you. The gift of hearing and knowing what is said. The gift of seeing accurately and far and the gift of using ears and eyes for judgment. Sight, hearing and true judgment – these are the gifts needed by every king and queen – you and I together in the Isle of the Waterfalls.

"This island is a place of birds and beauty just inland from the shore where you were camped. There are blue colored flowers and trees and jungle, flowing with streams of water and waterfalls, fountains and rainbows beam among leaves and rocks. I have a palace there for us to dwell in. It is a place for me to keep my beauty for you, if you will come to dwell with me. There is a bowl there filled up with the juice of blackberries to paint my eyebrows and my nails so black as you now see them. There are vats of grain fermenting for your joy in living. There are drinking horns and gold and silver cups all sparkling in the sun.

"There is a sunroom facing the southwest, neatly thatched with the wings and tails of many red-green birds. There are thick piles of river-rush for beds with coverings of blue-dyed wool and silks, whilst satins from the East cover the pillows. The walls are of bamboo covered with flowers and purple spiderwebs; the floors are green with ferns and docken leaves and meadow grasses.

"For each of us there is a throne of gold intricately inlaid with silver, studded with red and blue and gleaming gems. These high and oriental chairs are ringed around with birds singing in all the melodies of the rainbow.

"The people of my house, man-servants and maid-servants, are clean, healthy, well-dressed and groomed. Their hair is long and wavy like the manes of powerful horses chomping in the waves.

"The music that the birds sing in my palace would bring sleep to the eyes of tortured warriors suffering with the pain of broken bodies. The sweet calls of the thrushes and the larks, the blackbirds and the robins in the bushes, sing out for me and call me to the jungle. They call for me, 'Come here and join us, Sigh.'

"There is an orchard just beside my palace where there are vats of varied fruits and juices. There, trees of walnuts and blue mulberries grow with sweet-smelling leaves and apples and flowers. There also the bees build great hives of honey and from the streams the salmon, herring, bass and trout jump out into your hands. All these are in the gardens of my palace."

Whaleroarer and his warriors were stunned as Sigh sailed close then disappeared from view as her longboat shimmered and became a mist.

When the mist cleared, blown by the sea breezes, they saw an ancient hag of withered skin – Rivershark, with her long white hair, was laughing as the Mooncrow, cawing and calling, flew up into the air and perched upon a tree branch.

The Rivershark sneered and hid in the high tree watching the scene unfold of two great horses rearing up on their hind legs and snorting and beating with their hooves upon each other.

The vision was unclear and undulating but one horse was a White like Oceanhorse, the other was a Bay like Foresthorse. Now, in the vision, both were fighting fiercely and the Great White Stallion seemed to prevail. The Bay lay dead and many crows came down and flocked upon its body.   They feasted upon its red flesh while the witch, Rivershark, sat in the tree and laughed with Mooncrow.

Slowly the vision faded from their sight like an intruder spying and then hiding.

Then the fieldmarshal Whaleroarer gave orders to pull away from shore and navigate out to far distant lands where no delusions, where no mindmadness lurked to lure their vision.

Suddenly a cold storm blew and blocked their way. Great waves leapt up and screamed and waved their hands telling the warriornauts, "Get back, get back." Each wave was like an army and a barrier. They heard the sound of a thousand tramping feet blocking their way. The great waves heaved, threatening to smash the curragh into pieces, to drown Whaleroarer and his band of heroes.

Whaleroarer called upon his men, "Be brave. Join me in bailing out the wet green ocean."

They spread around the sides of their great boat and the curragh was bailed clear of salt sea water so that it floated but it rose up sideways, threatening to spill the heroes into the sea.

Fear fell on all and even the brave Whaleroarer, the fieldmarshal of the high-ground, cried aloud, "If only we were on dry land, I swear I could defend myself against any warrior but against an army of the sea, I cannot."

The turmoil of the ocean rocked the boat as the red and speckled salmon rose from the sand and shingle stones and leapt into the curragh. The warriornauts spread evenly around the curragh's sides and clung to them for balance to save them all from drowning in the ocean.

As they heaved up and down they saw far out the beautiful Sigh in her longboat, sails full, approaching over the sea waves.

As she cut close she shouted, "What would you give if I should save you all?"

The warriors replied, "What do we have that you would want?"

She answered, "Yourselves as my house warriors and protectors."

Whaleroarer and his men gladly agreed.

The Sigh sailed past them towards the Isle of Hills and all the seas beside her calmed and rested so that the heroes were able to follow her and row their curragh to a rivermouth that opened from the Isle of Waterfalls. Sigh left her narrow boat from the shore and welcomed them upon that golden strand.

Taking the hand of Whaleroarer, she led them along the stream bank where green hills swept down to the clear crystal waters flowing over the sandy riverbed of small white pebbles. The stream was silvery bright and in it swam red speckled salmon. All around were pleasant wild woods of singing birds flying about.

Whaleroarer told his sea-bred warriors, "Pull up our ship and dry it out and berth it. This would be a happy and a pleasant thing to live here always in the bird calls and in the sunshine."

As they walked in the woods, red serving girls came out bearing bright drinking horns of wines while others sat far off and played on reeds in a low background breeze of forest music.

Whaleroarer was pleased and told his troop of heroes, "This is the place where we can live forever."

They came to a wild orchard in the woods where the boughs were bending down with bright red apples. Scattered all around there were oak trees with green leaves and many acorn and hazel trees yellow with hazelnuts.

"It is summer here and yet at home it is still wintertime," said Whaleroarer.

His champions all agreed.

"It is true, as Sigh once promised us, this music from the birds that sing around us, would bring sleep to the minds of tortured warriors suffering from the pain of broken bodies."

And Sigh walked beside Whaleroarer as they climbed the hills that led to a great moor of flowers and bees and butterflies and honey where a white palace shone in the blue sunlight.

"What place is this Queen Sigh?" asked Whaleroarer.

"This is our home, where we can dwell in peace. Where I have lived alone with all my ladies since we first left the place where you come from – that dark unquiet land that is the world – here we can live forever in a better country."

CHAPTER NINE

A FIELDMARSHAL QUEEN BECKONS

Four buzzards flew down to the great snowy plain of the East country. They began to pick the dead that lay there after a skirmish between the Icedragon and the horsethieves that came from the West country.

Some horses had been stolen and some men had died upon the dusty buzzard plain. The brave fieldmarshal of the low country, all the gray plains and bushlands of the East, was Icedragon, head of the buzzard division.

Seeing the buzzards picking the dead bodies, some of the leading warriors of Icedragon muttered that this might be an omen of war, "Buzzards are often a symbol of death coming, sent by the powers of insight in the universe. The buzzard is the emblem of our division for we patrol and fight for bush and plains."

Icedragon nodded and assented, "In that case, this is an omen of a coming victory for all the four divisions of our army not just for our battalion. So be it."

Then the four buzzards disappeared from view giving way to the Four Witches of Kill. They were withered and stumbling, groaning and dithering as lean as death. These wrinkled and toothless hags, whose sagging skin fell loosely round their bones, beckoned and poked each other with their thin claws. Then the ground seemed to fall away beside them, opening up a vast underground plateau filled with rainbows and warm jungles of bushes. A wide road opened up through this dream landscape.

Icedragon led the way through in his chariot. Proudly and proprietarily he drove his splendid stallion by the groves of fruit and trees, beside the pleasant streams and crystal fountains.

In the far distance he could see the sea with the sun shining all around. This sunny island had appeared from nowhere out of a wide dusty plain of buzzards. Icedragon drove along his stallion who pranced and raised his legs and tossed his mane and tail and bowed and shook his head from side to side.

Icedragon glanced aside and saw two chariots, one on each side, riding along beside him. Each chariot was drawn by two bay horses just like the Great Red Bay of the Sternrider. The chariots were of wicker and steel with studs of silver and gold. Each of these two escorting chariots were driven by two warrior queens – one warriorwoman for each of the two bays.

These warrior queens wore armor, helmets and shields, along with all the accoutrements of combat. One of the warrior queens had eyes like meteors, just like the eyes of the witch Meteoreyes, just like two burning furnaces of fire. All four of these alert, well-armed and deadly warriorwomen were lithe and muscular. Each was tall, sharp, elegant and young-faced with thick and curly yellow hair flowing from underneath bronze helmets. All had nails like sharp black daggers at their fingertips. Their teeth were white as pebbles when they spoke.

One of the warrior queens spoke to Icedragon. Her eyes were grey-blue, calm and clear and thoughtful, not enflamed like meteors, "This is the Isle of Heroes and Amazons. Here you are welcome with your warriors. Here we perform heroic feats of arms, tricks of keen teamwork in the arts of war. Of course, if we should learn that our displays are needed in the real world by poor people, we are free to leave in order to right the wrongs of earth. But otherwise, does it not make sense to test and try our feats of heroism? Practicing to perfection all our jumps, our somersaults, our dirk throwing and duals.

"Our women warriors are well tried and tested but now they wish to practice against men so that we will surely come to be the fiercest Amazons in all the isles. All of your heroes may choose if he wishes to take a queen from any of our Amazons. Our fighting women all have serving girls who keep to household tasks and leave the queens free to study all the martial arts.

"My name is Smile and smiling is for joy or for wry wit and I can bring you both, if you should choose to take me as your queen. You are an icecold warrior with neither joy nor wit and it is known that most men worship all those fine qualities they do not have themselves. However, this is only for your choice whether to choose a queen whose personality is different from your own."

Icedragon replied coldly, "Tell us now, what are the ways of life in this strange place? Are acrobatic feats of combat all that I would do here?"

"Not at all, Icedragon, we eat only the best of fruits, nuts, fish and our bright sun brings life and health to all. Our warrior queens are fair as well as strong. Death and his friends, old age and pain and sickness, these four destroyers of the best Wavewarriors, we have locked out and barred from our bright island."

Icedragon asked the fieldmarshal queen, "And why has Death never been barred from earth?

Then Smile replied, "Death and his three friends, old age and pain and sickness, must live in the world. The earth is their inheritance since first man took his brother's life but here we do not live on earth but in a special landscape of mind and dreams. Here one exists in a mindscape that stretches from one man to another where a traveler can walk from one mind to another as in dreams.

"On this dream landscape time does not exist – it cannot kill us, it cannot destroy us, so we cannot grow old or wither away. Here, we live always in the present dream – our feet are planted firmly on this platform made of the magic footpath between minds. That is why some visions are prophetic and time is not present to tie down and confuse us on this rich wavelength of the dream jungles."

"Who holds the key to these dream worlds?" asked Icedragon.

"The key lies with the Four Witches of Kill – if you desire the mindscape you must find them to walk on that lone path from mind to mind, invade the mind of anyone and color it the way a child colors a blank color book."

Then Queen Smile turned her chariot to the West and her companion chariot went with her. Icedragon drove with them, his heroes followed. They drove through thick orchards and purple jungles. They galloped across the plain through rainbows and tall flowers. Then they arrived at the great fastness where Queen Smile ruled from her gemrich silver throne. Beside her throne stood a high golden chair which now was empty. There a thick mist fell down like the white pall that cloaks a palace when a great king comes home to shelter there on a winter's night. Around the fastness was a wall of bronze where the Icedragon rode his chariot over a silver drawbridge and through a gate of pearl.

The house within the bronze walk of the fastness was built of brown bricks and was carpeted with red and gold rugs of the Orient; the roof was thatched with the white wings of doves. The house was filled with strangely scented flowers that stung the nostrils. Then a mist appeared in a large hall where the two thrones stood.

While the Icedragon breathed in this strong smell, the mist changed into the form of the witch Landslink who writhed and transformed into a huge buzzard. As the mist wafted away she took the appearance of Queen Smile, a beautiful woman with golden skin and hair, clear and solid.

"Come sit upon this golden throne Icedragon. There I will show you visions of our Amazons of whom you could well become the great fieldmarshal."

She pointed towards the window where appeared a great battalion of Amazons dressed in the full accoutrements of war and riding upon gold chariots drawn by bays. Beside them stood a grove of hazel trees watered by a white stream. The nuts blew from the trees towards the Amazons, purple and yellow windfalls, which the warriors reached out and ate as their proud steeds drove by.

"Those are the hazel nuts of courage that are nourished by the warm river of honor and blown down by the winds of battle skill." Queen Smile told Icedragon. "In the distance, some of the chariots are dismounted and the horses set to graze in the woods of hazel trees while the Amazons battle in the hot waterfalls. Here, all the day, is sunlight and warm winds. Now our fieldmarshal comes to talk to us."

Suddenly, out of a mist in the great hall of thrones, there appeared a young woman with long yellow hair. She wore a silver helmet from which flowed her golden hair as thick as a lamb's wool. She wore a red cloak draped around her shoulders, a coat of silver mail with leggings of steel. Her left hand clutched five javelins. Around her waist she wore a belt and sword and on her back a shield with gemstones round the orle. In her right hand she grasped a five-barbed dart and pointed to the ranks of the Amazons.

She spoke to the Icedragon, "These warriorwomen could be yours, fieldmarshal, and I will work with you and the Queen Smile when the queen says the word. These warriorwomen have gone out to avenge the weak and honest against the greedy cruel warlords who devour the innocent – even high nobles have fallen before these beautiful Amazons. The blood of many highborn have been spilt and many widows of the mighty mourn and weep because their husbands and sweethearts have run away with the Other Woman – Death.

"Your emblem is the Buzzard. The buzzards hiss in your plains and gray bushlands and grizzled dark graveyards of dust and decay and decomposition. Here in the happy fields of sunshine there is purple fruit and laughter.

"These Amazons are beautiful in battle – see phalanx after phalanx drum ahead some Amazons on foot, some on great chariots – keen spears and javelins ready, shields on arms, swords at their waists, with dirks in their sleeves, black daggers on their painted fingertips. See deadly poisoned small-globes of sharp spikes swinging from every wrist. These fatal women have overcome all men who stood before them.

"These warriorwomen are far-seeing and understanding in the ways of war. Their lips are thin and grim, their teeth are filed, their eyes are sharp and pierce into the foe. Their arms and legs and shoulders swing and swerve in beautiful and deathly coordination.

"These muscular, lithe warriorwomen are good at killing men, good in the battle, cunning, good also at storytelling and in making songs. For they sing on the nights before a battle to warn the enemy and they sing after a battle to soothe the women and children of the dead. Theirs is the hum of deadly destiny that causes men and women to stop their ears and seek to run away. But there is nowhere that they can run to for their fate is sealed by those above them who have closed the door. These Amazons are feared for their grim dedication."

Then Smile addressed the Icedragon, "It would be dishonorable not to help these Amazons."

And Icedragon asked Queen Smile. "I do admire their weapons. From what strange nation do they buy their arms? I have never seen the like of their blue swords."

She replied, "Their arms come from the pit where demons smelt and forge their spears and swords and javelins. I get their weapons from the smithery of the pit itself. There the devils torture and capture young offspring of the devil and beat them, screaming and demented into the metals of their weapons. Fiends fly from daggers and dirks when they stab foes.

"Ghouls and hobgoblins howl from the hard shields where everywhere is a grinning face of satan. Demons scream from the spears and swords of Amazons and devils jump from their javelins of kill. Such weapons and such wives can soon be yours if all your heroes do agree to join us with our fieldmarshal.

"Is this agreed?" Smile asked.

Icedragon's men were pleased to give agreement.

"Is this enough to keep you here?" asked Smile.

Icedragon was still wary. "It is enough to try this place of paradise – this place of ease for a short time, at least."

CHAPTER TEN

BAD DREAMS AND SUMMERSAILOR

Summersailor was the fieldmarshal of the sky division. In the combat zone they carried the accoutrements of war from one part of the battle to another. Wherever chariots or horses, spears or swords, axes or javelins or dirks were needed, wherever anything had suffered damage, the Hawks fought their way through and delivered it. It was just like a free gift from the sky the warriors said.

Also, they fought their way through to move men from one part of a fierce fight to another. In this way, the balance of the battle could be changed to help their comrades on the day.

Summersailor was the brother of brave Waterbear and one of the senior vi-kings of the Seagulls. The hawk was the sign of these sky warriors.

One dark night, at the Castle of Summersailor, an old witchwoman visited.

She was dressed in a black cowl wrapped closely around her head. She drove a burnt black chariot that looked as though it had been driven through the pit and set on fire by demons. It was pulled by two black horses with red eyes of fire. Likewise the witch had eyes of fiery flame.

She told a gateman that she sold good luck.

The gatemen asked her, "How high is your price?"

She replied, "I ask only a prayer. I give only a blessing."

They were stunned and let her through into the inner courtyard. For she had let them smell her stinging flowers of evil mindmanipulation and illusion so that they feared her vengeance and bad luck. The witch was Meteoreyes, her stock in trade was the medicine of delusion and false dreams. She had a cage of songbirds from the devil. They sang a song of dreaming and mindmadness.

She lit a small fire just below the tower and burnt her flowers under the high windows. In the room above, the young Princess Whitehair lay fast asleep and smelled the devil flowers. The smoke that drifted upwards in the twilight carried hallucination and deceit.

When the small girl woke up and looked out of her high window she saw the sameshape of her uncle, the Summersailor. Her father was dead. Her mother was Purplelake, the sister of Waterbear, King of the Wavewarriors.

Whitehair had the gift of discerning spirits but was overcome by the visions and the sounds and the smell of the delusional smoke and flowers. Soon she was seized away in a sleepful haze.

***

At the same time, where Summersailor was asleep with his chief heroes and champions resting nearby, he was visited by a beautiful young Woman of the Sea who suddenly appeared before him smiling. "See, look behind you, women marching well with golden brooches shining on their tunics. Do not be fearful, mighty Summersailor. I will be sure to guide you on your way. My name is Laugh. I am a child of joy and laughter – I am a warriorwoman from the Isle of Farsky one of the Islands of the Everyoung.

"There is no weeping or mourning in that land. Truthtelling is there. When someone says I will meet you at such a place, at such a time, on such a day, you do not go there just to find that you are all alone. No treachery or doubledealing is used. No cheats or liars live there. There no one will rob you of your life's blood, for those who steal your time in this sad place are robbing you of life. Promises are kept. When married women pledge to love, that love is always true. Come with me to the happy Isles of Farsky.

"Do you remember how you got your name – brave Summersailor? When you were a child of only five you pleaded for the chance to sail alone and unaccompanied for you were living with your foster brothers, to toughen you and put you through the mill of poor and rough experience. Your foster family would not take this chance but spoke to your real father, who gave permission for you to sail alone and unaccompanied only in summer until you reached the age of ten. Then you would be allowed to sail in winter too.

"Then I and my hawk people watched you sail alone on the high seas, brave Summersailor. I so admired your courage that I swore that when you grew up I would visit you and offer you my heart – and this I do. Now some strange power has released me to make this long longed-for visit to entreat you."

Then Summersailor thought back to his boyhood. "I do remember that hawks flew overhead when I was a boy just learning to sail. Where do you come from?"

"I am a hawk, a seawoman. We live on Islands of the Everyoung. The sea is my blue garden grown with fruit. When you think that you are sailing on the sea, among the small green waves of summertime, I see a planted wood of birds and leaves when I drive out brightly in the sun upon my chariot pulled by sea-horses. You see the prow of your longboat through the snow-white waves throwing the spray about. I see only, as I ride the waves, fine fields with daisies growing all around. You see the wood of your longboat that smells like salt seaweed and makes you deeply sigh. I see a wood of hazelnuts and chestnuts surrounded by red flowers that smell of wine. I see the woods that will not pass away nor die to winter's blight of snow and cold.

"You see the seaweed growing in the deep dark mountains of the waves. I see only the high trees of the woods with leaves of gold and the gold flowers of the forest that will never be cut away by any mortal man. You see the crimson jellyfish that sting. I see the red roses in the paths of shrubs. I see the paths for feet that walk and ride the pathways of the sun that shine forever.

"Where you see warriorbirds that caw and prey, follow each other to destroy and kill, I hear the sound of blue and yellow birdlets chirping a greeting to the traveler. The birds I hear, I hear them this very minute, would make a sick man well, would soothe minds tormented by your fellow man, would heal trouble in any heart of turmoil or despair.

"These far birdsongs would heal you from all pain - would heal you from the darts of hate or envy. Will you join me in the Island of Farsky, as I have hoped and longed for since you were a small boy, fighting the waves to become a summersailor?

"The ageold waves throw spray against your boat like an old man with white hairs among the gray. I see the yellow herbs among the green in the thick grasses of the wood. You see the black seal swimming out to watch your boat. I see only young golden maidens dance in flowers, gold-yellow horses prancing in the fields. You see dark dreams of turmoil and dismay. I see blue visions of white hills and sun."

So Summersailor strode into her chariot where a strange transformation seized him and he felt younger and his sight more sharp and all around were happy, cheerful faces of the hawk people and his own friends and champions. Proudly the horses pranced. The chariots rocked backward and forward over the green waves of grass and soil and flowers of the sea. This was just as the Queen of Laugh had promised. The seahorses shook their manes and bowed and flicked their tails from side to side as they took the Summersailor and his chief heroes to the land of Farsky in the purple jungles of the Everyoung, to live for evermore.

CHAPTER ELEVEN
WHITEHAIR AND THE WITCHES

On that same night, in the Castle of Summersailor, the servants saw that the fieldmarshal had gone with all his champions. The gray wrinkled witch spread out simple flowers and the small girl, Whitehair, saw what she thought to be the form and shape of Summersailor. So the gray witch led the child out into the black chariot pulled by a pair of coal black stallions. This took them to the Castle of Warwords in the distant woods where the Four Witches of Kill still lived and schemed.

At once the child Whitehair was bound with chains and locked away in the cellar of the castle to remain there until Whitehair was needed to be a hostage. Or until she grew up to be used to receive a transplant of the brain of Meteoreyes – to bring new life and a new body to that Witch of Kill.

Likewise, three other girls were held as captive for the same purpose by the other witches. The Witches of Kill spread out the rumor that all the girls were sacrificed and dead. No one would doubt this. So the witches were prepared to work their devilcraft after the term of their natural and normal life was over – beware of young ladies who look innocent.

After they had locked the girls away, with fear by day and black dreams in the night, the Four Witches of Kill stoked up the fires that had been built with the bones of victims.

Landslink addressed the others, "It is time for the Hillwolves to launch the war against the Wavewarriors, now that the chief heroes of the Wavemasters have been taken away. Not one of them knows where the others are, nor cares. Now that they live afar in Isles where all is happy, where no war disturbs the tranquil mind – what favors we have brought!

"Let us send messengers to Snakeknife and Warchariot, telling them it is safe to launch attacks that will steal all the warhorses from the East leaving their chariots to rot and rust. They need only to hold hard to Seaspear for Waterbear to become isolated. For what can one man do against an army?"

At that time, Gentleleaf, the queen of Seaspear, pleaded with Seaspear to desert Warchariot.

However, Snakeknife and Warchariot told Seaspear, "You hold all the seapower – all the ships both theirs and ours are under your command. Just keep them neutral – we will not interfere. We will not break our word to you, brave Seaspear – pay no attention to a bunch of horsethieves. Even the Sternrider is under our control. Nothing has changed between us. Let us keep our bargain just as we agreed. You are the sole and absolute fieldmarshal of all ships."

Seaspear replied, "If that should change, I will change sides."

"We know. That is why we have always said, stay and make sure that all our warships cannot be used against your people. What could be more fair?"

But Gentleleaf wept many times and pleaded with Seaspear not to trust the Hillwolf king and queen.

Then Seaspear answered, "I trust only myself."

And Gentleleaf replied, "I know you will be neutral but a leader of men should never trust in himself but only in the rules – the first rule says to be one of a good team."

So Seaspear chose to go on ruling all ships under Warchariot's ultimate kingship. But still Seaspear was restless and disturbed in sleep and in his walks from dream to dream.

CHAPTER TWELVE
ALONE AT THE STRAITS

Waterbear stood alone in his chariot, with only his attendants and horse servants, beside the straits that link up East and West. There at the sign of cria and the sea, at low tide, this became a sandy isthmus.

His four fieldmarshals and their leading heroes had gone to seek a long life in the dream jungles of the far western Isles of the Everyoung.

His sister Gentleleaf had gone to join Seaspear in his sailing ship where he was now fieldmarshal of all seamen.

The Queen Springvision, mother of Wallwave, had gone to take her young son Stormbolt to foster with the Kim family and to join his elder brother, the young boy Wallwave, in training for the feats and skills of combat.

Purplelake, sister of Summersailor, was a widow who had no one to help her find young Whitehair. Nevertheless, Purplelake had gone to find that missing daughter Whitehair, who had last been seen with the witch Meteoreyes. For Meteoreyes created mindmadness and illusion. Indeed, when Whitehair had been lured away, she saw the dark image of Meteoreyes as her uncle, the Summersailor.

So brave Waterbear fought alone. There beside him stood the Great White Stallion - the Oceanhorse, strong and loyal and war-skilled.

Warchariot gathered together all his Hillwolf army into the thick bushes west of the swift straits.

Waterbear stalked at night among that army, killing and mutilating and beheading among the war camps of the gathering foes. He sowed the seeds of terror in the darkness. So the Hillwolves became fearrattled and bone-jittery.

Then Seaspear heard a rumor that the horses of the East were going to be stolen. He sent a warning to the Waterbear. So Waterbear secretly sent some of his horse servants to drive away and hide as many horses as they could so that the horsethieves of Warchariot would flee away empty handed.

To get back to their army, the five horsethieves had to pass over the swift straits between East and West. They knew that Waterbear was nearby, so they hid in the forest until the king would sleep. Then Waterbear sent his servants out to find them and point them out. But crias flew overhead and swooped down on the heads of the horsethieves, crying aloud and showing their exact location. Waterbear threw his javelins and transfixed four of the horsethieves to the trees, cutting their heads off with his battle axe.

The fifth horsethief surrendered to Waterbear, who told him, "Line the heads up on your chariot, stick them upon the spikes along the back. In this way, they will grin and grimace to the crowds of Hillwolves as you drive through your camp. Drive them right through the soldiers of your army until you reach the campsite where your Queen Snakeknife sits with King Warchariot. There they sit, unaware of danger, under the roof of shields held by their bodyguards. Until you do so I will stand upon that rock and watch you. If you do not deliver, you will receive this javelin through your chest. I want the Hillwolves and their king and queen to see what I have set aside for them."

The fifth horsethief assured Waterbear, "I swear I will deliver your true message."

The horsethief drove his chariot over the straits, the chariot horse tossing his mane and tail just like the flying foam on either side into the bushland of the Hillwolf armies.

But when the surviving horsethief with the severed heads reached his friendly front battalion, he felt at home and safe among his fellows. And, not wanting to display the severed heads as a boasting for the deadly Waterbear, he left his chariot with the heads aloft and ran to meet his fieldmarshal Sternrider.

However, he fell down prostrated on his face, his hands almost touching the leader's feet, his face screwed up with blood, his mouth gasping, his chest pinned down with the sharp javelin of Waterbear who did what he had promised.

Sternrider bore the message to the Snakeknife who quietly muttered to King Warchariot, "We cannot win while Waterbear is there – he bars our way, whether his island lies as low-tide isthmus or as high-tide straits. For when the tide is high it rushes freely, sweeping along the warboats and the skiffs. And when the tide is low it drains away and leaves a path of sand where only one warrior at a time may pass, such is the slippery nature of that path. Coming or going is for him to say. If we would steal their warhorses as planned, we must remove Waterbear from the straits. But who will now be forced to face this madness? Who wants to stand against a man who fights alone and singlehanded against the mightiest army in the world? Who would stand up in single combat against a solitary hero like the Waterbear."

Sternrider answered, "I will find a man who is skilled and honorable and a man of courage or a warrior who is seeking to make his name, a gloryseeker who needs to be a winner, a cool blade who would fight a rabid lion."

"You are very wise Sternrider," said Snakeknife.

When Sternrider went to seek out his best champions, Snakeknife muttered to the king, "Sternrider is too direct and honest. We don't need a champion to fight the Waterbear. We need a crew of sly and cunning killers. Let us call upon the help of the Queen of Justice, for surely her friends are sleekit, sharp, dirk throwers."

The Justice Queen gathered around her many vile disguisers who were skilled in the secret arts of assassination and then she released them upon brave Waterbear.

***

Waterbear stood alone in his chariot in the middle of the slow green seaweeded sea with sand and bushes and a gray shrubbery lying all around on both sides of the isthmus.

The friends of the Justice Queen were indeed deadly, each one with cunning swiftness and disguises. Each one came dressed as a sand dune slitherer and slow crawler - python, boar, fawn, fox and giant gray rat and wolfhound who slunk around and skulked among the sand and shrubbery, ready to sneak upon the Waterbear and spear him.

Unluckily for these quiet and still assassins, crawling their way along the grassy sandunes, the crias were crying aloud in fear above them. For the crias discerned only the smell of man, the world's most deadly animal, now treading among their hidden eggs and sand nests. They swooped down and hit the heads of each disguised assassin and, as the crias swooped and screamed and hit, the Waterbear shot each assassin dead with an arrow shot from his deer hunting bow. There they lay, slithery, cunning and bushwise but now as dead as any simple trout.

While Waterbear was dealing with these attacks, other Hillwolves rode by and stole some horses. So Waterbear cried out to the Sternrider, "Send out to me one warrior who has the courage to fight me face-to-face, one at a time in one-to-one combat. All your disguisers can easily be seen by the small birds who fear for their sand nests. I will allow your forces to advance, even to steal some horses from us but only as long as the one-to-one combat lasts."

Sternrider approached the straits in his chariot. Politely he nodded with respect to great Waterbear, "Waterbear, my greetings go to you. Please know that these disguised and cunning killers were not sent by me – that is not my form. Those slinking assassins were sent to you by the strange seer known as Justice Queen who did predict a victory for her friends."

Waterbear laughed aloud.

Sternrider smiled, "I fear that war is building up between us in spite of all our honorable efforts. Your four fieldmarshal's taking leave of you and going to live in dreams, appears to many to have destroyed your army. You are defenseless but I will find a warrior worthy of you, as you have asked. One who will not need cunning, one who will combat with you man-to-man.

CHAPTER THIRTEEN

THREE VETERANS OF COMBAT

Three fierce and powerful warriors stood before Queen Snakeknife and the King Warchariot. These warriors were the three Drumnecks, veterans of combat. The three were brothers. They looked exactly like each other with their battlegear, armor, helmets and their black cloaks. Three gorillas, hairy and ugly, bony and odorous, were never more alike.

Sternrider, the fieldmarshal of the Hillwolves, bowed low before the king and queen, "My sovereigns, here I present three brothers for the battle against the hopeless and alone, brave Waterbear. They have agreed to fight him man-to-man, one at a time, no ganging up on him, all single combat.

"In return, Waterbear has agreed that, while they struggle on, our armies will be free to press ahead – perhaps for three days. Otherwise, no one would come to stand against him and he would never have a chance to defeat us and defend the East from our fierce Hillwolf warriors. It is better for us to lose one man at a time rather than to be destroyed with heavy losses, for his swift sword would soon mow down large numbers of our men, ten at a time. Waterbear will not try to stop us while we round up the horses of the great East that we had planned to take out of the way of combat and battle."

Warchariot and the queen were pleased and pleasant, "After we have the horses, we must win even if all their fighting force returns from what seems foolishness across the sea – the search for the Islands of the Everyoung."

Warchariot and the Snakeknife shook their heads. "What caliber of men would leave their friends, their families and their country and their king for such a craze of dreams and mind delusions? It cannot be too difficult to win against such simplehearted, superstitious seamen who only know and trust the ocean – a trust misplaced, if ever there was one.

"Only the boy Wallwave can control the sea and he is still in early training. So you have only to kill Waterbear. Of course, I speak only in general terms. I feel sure that you will kill the Waterbear but do not underrate his powers of kill.

"It would give heart to others to go against him if you could even touch the eastern shore after your battle. Even if a warrior won such a token victory and died, his memory and his family would be honored. For wars are won by many such small gestures."

Displeased with these words, the eldest Drumneck spoke with arrogance, "I have no intention of leaving my body anywhere. I intend to leave the bones of Waterbear out there and to come home alone, receiving honors, as I have always done in times gone by."

Sternrider and the king and queen were eager to calm the pride of the Drumnecks. They nodded in sure approval, "But, of course, you shall have honor, popular acclaim, a writing of approval and gallantry, fine words of praise on a small plaque of bronze signed in engravement by the king and queen."

The three Drumnecks set their faces hard against Waterbear. They were pleased and strode away like three cocks strutting in the early morning to cock-a-doodle-do at the first dawn.

After the three cocks had strutted out, the Great Bay horse ridden by Sternrider crossed over the straits and hid, ready and waiting. He drove a great herd of horses led by the Great White Stallion over the straits from East to West. These stolen horses were then hidden away to be used later in the coming war campaign with chariots, against the Wavewarriors.

Seaspear observed this horseraid from far off but could not sail in time to intervene.

***

A great crowd of the curious, hopeful Hillwolves gathered to watch the contest between the three Drumnecks and the Waterbear.

The Drumnecks, breaking their word that they would fight one at a time in single combat, now threw themselves in fury at the Waterbear.

Two strode in front, holding their shields to hide the third who sneaked upon the Waterbear with a great axe. The two with shields, holding a grip of spears and javelins, then ran one to each side, one north the other south. Waterbear turned his chariot with speed just as the spears and javelins were flying so that they tore into the chariot's backboard. At the same time the Waterbear jumped out into the shallow waters of the strait. He leapt upon the Drumneck, who wielded the axe, cutting his head off with a sword. Then Waterbear seized a spear out of the backboard of his chariot and flung it through the heart of number two. The third Drumneck rushed forward with his sword but Waterbear threw his broad sword with such force that it went through the shield and body armor into the heart of Drumneck number three.

As number three splashed around bleeding and dying, he screamed out to the terrified observers, "I claim the eastern shore, though I am dying. All of you can come later to fulfill my claim. See this left hand of victory and in my good right hand a sword of war."

The Drumneck splashed and crawled upon the shore of the Eastland and died, clutching the soil. The Waterbear walked over in his fury and severed the hands and feet of the Drumneck who made the arrogant claim to victory. Likewise, he cut off both the hands and feet of the other Drumnecks who had broken faith and threw them all into his chariot.

He drove his chariot to the Hillwolves shore and smeared it all around with gumtree syrup then covered it with dead seaweed and branches and dried leaves all around the top and sides and back of its wood canopy.

Then Waterbear set fire to the whole chariot and drove it fiercely through the camp of Hillwolves and threw the hands and feet of the Drumnecks onto the ground beside the main campfire, crying out, "Those who wish to follow the war claim of the Drumnecks, let him know that the same fate awaits him as these hands who cannot hold and the same fate awaits him as the poor feet that cannot walk the earth."

Then he drove back his fiery chariot as Snakeknife and King Warchariot declared, "The three Drumnecks have honor, popular acclaim – a writing of approval and gallantry to be inscribed upon a plaque of bronze."

But those who heard these words were silent and evasive as they stood beside the sea, watching the crias.

CHAPTER FOURTEEN
SNAKEKNIFE SNARLS BACK

Warchariot and Snakeknife called a conference, with Seaspear and Sternrider, to find a way to deal with Waterbear.

Sternrider said, "So far I have tried hard to keep our conflict honorable and just. I am sorry that the three champions we sent against the Waterbear were frauds and losers. Seaspear, you have a foot in both our camps. Why don't you choose a seaman who is fair, who would be fierce enough to fight the Waterbear."

The Seaspear shook his head, "I am impartial. Waterbear is my friend; my task is only to keep this war from getting any worse. We must try to reverse this enmity before both Hillwolves and Wavewarriors destroy each other. Let us have a truce – a time for talk where both sides can back off. This is a raging river that hurtles on in torrents and in turmoils. Let us stop it before it comes to death dealing in thousands."

"I do agree," said Snakeknife, "but men cannot or will not do the talking. I will meet with one of their main warriorwomen and try to calm the raging river waters into a smoothly flowing gentle stream."

All four agreed.

Seaspear was pleased and added, "The sister of Summersailor, sweet Purplelake, will be back in a few days from her search to find Whitehair."

"Has that child wandered off?" asked Snakeknife, cunning friend of the Four Witches of Kill who had kidnapped and held Whitehair in chains.

Seaspear replied, "That young girl has the gift of being able to discern dark spirits – only strong magic could have stolen her. There is also the queen of Waterbear, my sister, Springvision. She is wise in words and would be glad to talk about a truce, though she is fiery and impetuous – a warriorwoman quick to throw a javelin."

Queen Snakeknife frowned and shook her head and thought. "When she returns from searching for her child perhaps I could truce-talk with Purplelake. Until then, we must find a warrior to hold the battle against Waterbear. So you, Seaspear, send us some of your best men of the Hillwolves and we will choose between them so that there will be no conflict for you. No Wavewarrior will go against the Waterbear."

Seaspear did so but worried and was uneasy.

"No man alive could stand against the Waterbear," he told the king and queen.

They nodded politely.

Sternrider, too, was thoughtful and disturbed.

The seaman chosen was Gripstone the Hillwolf who was promised his own fighting ship after he had addressed the king and queen.

"Mere medals, praise and popularity are fine but do not necessarily last over the years. I need a home that I can defend in the face of thieving foes – a place to call my own – a place that no one can take away from me – a fighting ship with the firm loyalty of warrior seamen. I need a ship to attack the Waterbear; I cannot merely splash around in water. He has a chariot and the Great White Stallion – or a like horse – to thunder and to plunder, to cut us into pieces, scatter our bones and yell and shout in defiance at our armies."

"This could be good for us as well as you," agreed the Warchariot. "You shall have a ship from which to attack the Waterbear. If the ship is damaged in the fierce combat, then you shall have another when you return. Then I will raise you to the rank of vi-king to show the world you are an honored champion."

The Hillwolf warrior was well pleased and bowed humbly before the king and queen, "Thank you."

Then Gripstone went to supervise his ship. It was to be rowed by Hillwolf warriors. Inside the ship were weapons such as swords and daggers, javelins and spears, bolt-driven bows and slings, loud singing shields that screamed a warning when the foe came near.

The Queen of Justice also spoke to Gripstone to encourage him to take part in the combat. She made a false prophecy, "It is foredoomed that the Waterbear will fall.

Here is a parrot that repeats my words from far away so if my foresight changes it will inform you. You will be forewarned."

Gripstone was happy to receive the parrot and tied it to his shoulder strap. It cawed and croaked, "The Waterbear will die before Gripstone."

When Gripstone sailed his longboat into the straits at the high tide, Sternrider sent his thieves across the sea to round up herds of horses hidden among the bushes and the forests.

While brave Waterbear waited alone for Gripstone at the straits, he saw several crows fly up in the far distance. He knew that they had been disturbed and frightened by the hooves of sudden moving herds of horses. Because he had to make a firm stand against Gripstone, there was nothing more that Waterbear could do to stop the horsethieves driving off the stallions.

But Waterbear was helped by the fierce seas that rose up. It was as though those seas knew that Waterbear was in need as they came to the defense of the father of the Wallwave. The waves turmoiled into a mighty wall of combat to drive back all the stallions and the horsethieves.

It is strange how nature sometimes echoes the person. Nature is often in full harmony with man.

Then Waterbear stepped back from the great waves and threw two javelins. One of the javelins went through the parrot that perched on the shoulder of Gripstone while it shouted, "The Waterbear will die before the Gripstone."

The other javelin pieced the steering wheel and sank deep into the hard wooden deck of Gripstone's ship, locking the wheel in place so that the ship could not be steered in time to master the high waves. The ship was doomed to crash against the nearby rocks. It perished and all the weapons fell to the sea bottom and sank into the sand.

The seamen swam back to the western shore and told the king, "The weather was against us; the seas rose despite the good predictions of the parrot given us by the Justice Queen."

Warchariot sneered, "Only a fish would trust a parrot." He ordered the wrecked seamen to be beheaded.

***

Now Gripstone also swam to the western shore after his ship was wrecked upon the rocks. But he stood firm against the Waterbear and called to him across the straits, "Come choose your weapons, for you are the only one who has been challenged."

The Waterbear sat high upon his chariot drawn by two seahorses, prancing and plunging; their manes and tails swishing and flowing like the salt sea foam that flies and sprays the air.

"You have lost most of your weapons in the sea but I will give you what you need," said Waterbear.

"I want nothing from you except your life," replied Gripstone. "Now choose your deadly weapon."

"If I could have my choice, I would choose my hands and wring your neck – it is so stiff and arrogant," said the Waterbear.

Gripstone replied, "No weapons are the best weapons of all; no armor is the best protection, too, for that will make us all the more determined to see the best man win at hand-to-hand."

The Mooncrow screeched and cawed in hatred as both left their weapons and armor on the shore and plunged into the sea. A slithery seasnake was set loose by the Mooncrow upon Waterbear. It wound itself around his legs and tripped him so that he fell backwards just as Gripstone was flinging himself forward at brave Waterbear. As the Gripstone fell forward and lost his balance, Waterbear was able to seize him by the throat and throttle him with both hands under the water.

Waterbear stood up and tore the seasnake off, holding it up and crushing it in his hand. He threw it at the Hillwolf camp and shouted, "Here is a dead snake, take it to your live one."

But no Hillwolf did, for fear of the Snakeknife.

Waterbear took up his accoutrements of war and armed himself for battle against the horsethieves. He drove his chariot towards the circling crows. For now that the waters were abating somewhat, the thieves were still trying to round up horses and drive them over the straits to join the Hillwolves. The horses chomped and neighed and near stampeded among the trees and bushes to escape the cruel whips and goads of the horsethieves.

The crows and other birds were still disturbed and flocking high and circling over the trees. Waterbear could see them up above the trees and bushes and soon he fell upon the horsethieves. He slew them swiftly, letting one escape to tell the story to their king – Warchariot.

Then Waterbear drove his chariot to his ship. He sailed away to join Springvision and Purplelake in a hidden faroff fastness. In the absence of the champions of the Wavewarriors, the stronghold was secured only by armed and arrowed servants.

These things were then reported to Snakeknife who called a meeting with her Justice Queen.

The king and Snakeknife were beside themselves, outraged and furious at the Waterbear. "We have an army, the greatest in the world and one man takes our strategy apart. We need to get their horses on our side in case their champions should return to fight. This Waterbear can read the signs of nature and act like a small army on his own!

"So Waterbear has sailed away. I knew it. Let him return with weapons and body armor. No more splashing around with water wrestling. We need to match him with a deadly warrior. Nor have your omens helped us, Justice Queen. You need to use your brains, think of a plan."

"Of course and I will do so, Queen Snakeknife. I did not dare to offer you advice but I will do so if the Queen desires it. It would be bad if we should lose our hostage, young Whitehair. Her mother, Purplelake, is still distraught and determined to find her daughter. If I could say that you had found clues to the whereabouts of Whitehair, a quiet and secret meeting could be arranged between Queen Snakeknife and Purplelake, somewhere unknown to Waterbear. Also do we need more horses?"

"Of course not," replied Snakeknife, "but we need to keep the horses out of the way of the Wavewarriors in case their heroes should return."

Then the Justice Queen advised Queen Snakeknife, "Then kill the horses. Why should we kidnap these four-footed beasts. This puts us to great trouble and expense for nothing. Waterbear cannot drive away dead horses."

Queen Snakeknife shook her head, "You have exposed me as a mere softie. I am not ruthless enough; I swear that I will try to be more cruel. Of course the horses will be killed in future. Set up the meeting between me and Purplelake."

***

Unknown to the Waterbear, Purplelake walked into the snare laid out and slyly set by the false prophetess, the Queen of Justice. The fly was Purplelake, the spider was the Queen Snakeknife who laid the cunning trap.

The Queen of Justice came to visit Purplelake late after dark and spoke to her in secret, "I think that Queen Snakeknife knows all about the disappearance of your daughter Whitehair who is being held hostage. If the war goes badly for the Hillwolves, Whitehair may be exchanged for a queenly sum of money. Warriors can solve things only with the force of arms but we ladies are more subtle and devious. Snakeknife is mainly interested in wealth. Perhaps you could pay more for Whitehair than the price demanded by the King Warchariot and so get back your daughter now. I also need a small fee for my services."

Purplelake paid Justice Queen her small fee and went with her by night and in secret, though curious servants listened at the door.

Now Purplelake was very tired and desperate after her long search to find Whitehair with no good outcome. So she foolishly went with Justice Queen to speak to the Snakeknife.

In a bright moonlit clearing in the woods, where the Snakeknife had hidden ambushers and assassins, the sly Queen Snakeknife spoke to Purplelake, "Are you still searching for your daughter Whitehair? Are you still trying to persuade the Waterbear to hunt for Whitehair, even to battle for her?"

"Never will I give up until I find her. I will keep looking for her till the day I die."

"That is so sad," said Snakeknife, "I feared as much, poor mother. Now I must bring your misery to an end."

And Queen Snakeknife signaled to the javelineers who stood by in the shadows of the moonlight.

CHAPTER FIFTEEN
QUEEN OF JUSTICE

Waterbear slept uneasily and awoke like a prisoner breaking out of a black dungeon, swam in the seaweed like a seal in summer, then decked himself in the accoutrements of war. Like a cock striding out in the cold dawn he saw, far from the straits, grey forms of buzzards descending out of dull clouds – the scavengers of death, circling around and waiting for a chance to swoop upon their prey and eat the bodies.

Six buzzards were prepared to come down upon a scene of slaughter and desecration. When he untied the Great White Stallion, it broke away and galloped to the scene of death from which the smoke curled slowly upwards. Waterbear followed the Great White Stallion, harnessing black and grey horses in his battle chariot. When Waterbear arrived at the scene of the buzzards, the Great White was stampeding at the head of a large herd of horses who had panicked to escape the spears and javelins of the horsethieves.

The horsethieves had been told to kill the horses and many broken bodies of fine animals were lying there – the victims of the spears. As the escape stampede galloped away, led by the White, some of the thieves and murderers were crushed to death by the hooves of the wild stallions. Far away the Great Bay horse retreated, abandoning his sortie on the horses of the East as he had tried to block their path.

The horsethieves had been hacking at an oak to block the road of access to the scene of death. Even as the oak tree fell across the path, Waterbear rode his horses high and cleared the oak tree, chariot and all, crashing and clattering on the other side.

The horse assassins fled away. Then Waterbear beheaded each of them. As they yelled and screamed, begging for mercy, one of the horse murderers cried aloud, "We only did what Justice Queen commanded."

Then a light snow stream fell upon the bodies of men and horses, like the pall that covers a palace when a king draws near to it on a winter's night.

Then Waterbear in his chariot followed the horses who had been led to safety by the White. He paused and looked back at the men and horses who lay there dead under the pall of snow. Slowly the buzzards circled down and fell upon their prey; their meal was now the richer for the sour taste of human murderer. Like the dark clouds that block the light of day, the buzzards slowly winged around in dryness and settled on their snow-flaked carcasses.

***

Seaspear still wanted a just end to war – a peace talk to bring honor to both sides. But Gentleleaf, his queen, spoke to Seaspear, "There is no such thing as an honorable war, for the broken crawl around on wounded knees. Close comrades treachery against each other, brother stabs brother in the back, the father sends spears through his son. Javelins spin out of control and kill the friend of years. War never is a war against the foe. All war is war against your friends and family.

"Whitehair, the child of Purplelake, my friend, is captured somewhere in the spiders' lairs of the Four Witches of Kill. The witches have said that Whitehair is dead but I do not believe their lies. She has a sixth sense and is useful to them – they only kill to gain direct advantage. Purplelake, too, is missing from her home and there are whispers that she went away with Justice Queen to search for her lost daughter. You have been trapped with one foot in each camp."

Seaspear replied to Gentleleaf, "I will go and speak to Snakeknife and Warchariot and make it clear whose army I support."

Seaspear then went to talk to Queen Snakeknife and said, "I wish to speak to you of Waterbear. He is my friend and comrade and I trust him as a strong warrior who cannot be defeated. Let us back off this war on Waterbear. No good can come of it. We cannot win. No man is harder to deal with than he. No point of sword or dagger is more sharp. No one is fiercer than the Waterbear, not a lion or tiger, no raven is more flesh-loving. No hammer is harder as a weapon of destruction. No door that opens out to war is closed more firmly than when he is standing there. He is skilled, well trained and seething for the fight. When he speaks out, the power of his voice tremors and timbers through the air. It brings alive the hero-light that flashes around him, setting a doom for those who stand before him. He shows the toughness of his sinewy muscles. It shows his valor, his hard-hitting arms, the rage and anger of his fierce killfury. His speed, his pride, his madness in the fight – victory must be his in the final battle."

But Snakeknife cried, "No way. He is one body. He can be wounded. He gets tired. He sleeps. He can be overcome – omens have told us. Also, the four great heroes of the Waves, the finest fieldmarshals of the Wavewarriors, with all their crack battalions by their side, are eating salmon and drinking strong red wine far in the Islands of the Everyoung. They sing and feast on the venison of courage. Yet they have raised no hand to strike against us. The victory could be ours if only we could find one man to move aside and crush the Waterbear. One man to kill one man – is that too much to ask?"

Seaspear replied, "It is not up to me to choose a man. I am only an admiral to guide longboats; to help seamen with skills of seamanship. Ask your advisor the Queen of Justice if she chooses to meet with Queen Springvision, to trucetalk with her. It may be that peace will triumph – unless you wish to talk of peace yourself. I take your point that men obsess with winning."

But Snakeknife feared that word of all her murders would soon leak out and she chose not to go, in case someone took vengeance for her crimes.

So Seaspear sent word to the Queen of Justice to come and talk and visit with Springvision. The Queen of Justice was troubled and unsettled and sent to Mooncrow for a read of omens. Mooncrow flew down and took the form of a hag, an ancient, shaking, moaning and trembling crone. Her face and skin were wrinkled and gray and withered. She led a monkey with her, ugly and strange. She offered Justice Queen three vials of foresight.

"First of all drink these vials of prophecy, then take this monkey of prognosis with you and keep it on your back."

Justice Queen drank and let the monkey climb up on her shoulder. At once she saw a vision of dead horses – the view that Waterbear had seen earlier.

"The omen is not good," she told Seaspear. "I have seen a vision of the two great stallions, only this morning, where the Great Bay Horse was driven away by the Great White Stallion. Dead horses of the East lay all around. I fear that Waterbear is sweating fire and soon will fly up into a killfury. When he killfuries he will kill all against him, even women."

"Prophecies are not always true," said Seaspear, "and I swear that if the Waterbear or any man even tries to wound you, I will take his head." But yet he spoke of male assassins only and did not think of women warrior queens.

"Will you ride beside me in your chariot to keep the peace with Waterbear?"

Seaspear then swore, "I will and I will send them word that I am coming."

CHAPTER SIXTEEN
REVENGE OF SPRINGVISION

When Springvision received this word from Seaspear of his coming, she dressed in body armor and full weapons of self-defense like a true warriorwoman including a hard shield which no sharp javelins could pierce.

Then she spoke to the Waterbear, "I must defend. I will not become another Purplelake. After she went at dead of night to talk to the Justice Queen, her body was found like any pincushion with javelins for pins. Stand by in case you want to talk of truce."

Seaspear arrived in his chariot with the Queen of Justice. He left his chariot and went to speak with Waterbear.

The Queen of Justice held a round shield before her and on her back the monkey of prognosis clung with its arms tightly around her throat. As they stood at the back of Seaspear's chariot, the monkey grinned and flashed its fine white teeth.

The Queen of Justice then addressed Springvision, "We need to speak of peace."

Then the Springvision carefully and deliberately selected her sharpest javelin and threw it swiftly through Justice Queen and the monkey, pinning them hard to the backboard of the chariot. As the sharp weapon fatally pierced her heart, the seer gave a loud gasp and clutched the javelin as though she needed its support to stand. Before she died she spoke with her last breath. The demons of the air, the fiends of war and the strange twisted cries of wayward weapons gone astray screamed out and then fell silent.

"Why did you do this?" asked the deadly seer, "before I had a chance to speak of peace."

"Because of Purplelake. Because of the dead horses - those brave and obedient warhorses that were willing to risk their lives just to help us in the battle. But you had them most cruelly destroyed to stop you raising more false hope to send men to their death. Then speak of peace, for now you die of war," Springvision answered her.

The Queen of Justice shook her head, "Those deaths were determined before life's years began – a thousand nights before the sun first shone. Death was their destiny as it is for all. I never claimed to be a truthful prophet. I claim only to be the Queen of Justice. I helped to bring about only the deaths of those who went to war unrighteously. I caused the fall only of those who deserved to die. My only victim was Queen Purplelake. That was my only unjust death. That was the first mistake I made and it destroyed me. My second great mistake was to trust Seaspear. He is not false or even duplicitous. He is divided in his loyalties and truly does not know which road to walk."

Then she fell forward a little, revealing that the monkey was still stuck upon the board, its mouth and eyes still staring.

Seaspear came back from his talk with Waterbear and mounted his chariot without a word. He sighed and grimly shook his head as he drove back to the Hillwolf camp with the monkey and the seer still shaking and transfixed upon the backboard of his chariot.

Waterbear asked Springvision, "Why did you do it?" and she replied, "I did not think it right that you, a hero, should have killed a prophetess and what else could we do with her, I ask you?"

Then Waterbear threw out his javelin at random into the nearby camp of Warchariot. It pierced Warchariot's ancient mother, Spiderlair, a sick old woman sitting in her wheelchair taking the sun. This brought great fear and trembling among the Hillwolf warriors. "He will kill all of us, women and all, if we allow him."

After this there was consternation and turmoil throughout the battle campgrounds of the Hillwolves.

***

After the death of Spiderlair, the Snakeknife searched desperately for a warrior who would challenge the Waterbear. At last she found Winterfire, the eldest son of Winterwarrior her deputy fieldmarshal. He agreed to challenge Waterbear. He was a fine, highly-skilled and honorable warrior. But Waterbear shook and trembled in a fury and took on the appearance of a bear. Waterbear stood before the young warrior and beheaded him as easily as though he took the head off a young fox caught stealing chickens.

The Waterbear called out, "Send me a man to stand alone before me. I want no more old women or young pups, no more horsethieves or cowardly horse murderers. Send me five men at once or even ten."

Then Queen Snakeknife sent out ten warriors in full armor with swords and helmets. Each held a spear that they flung at the Waterbear with deadly aim. Then Waterbear again took on the shape and likeness of a bear as he killfuried in a fit of rage. The Waterbear caught ten spears on his shield, mounted his chariot and swung his sword, the short thick sword that hacked its way through arms and legs and necks. He slashed and cut all ten like a great butcher cutting up ten pigs.

Then Warchariot became disorientated and shook from head to toe. He unscrewed his index finger with the long sharp nail and told his warriors, "Be firm and do not yield, for now the Waterbear has found killfury, his herolight is shining like a halo and he berserks and turmoils in his mind. I wish that we had not destroyed his horses nor even allowed you, Snakeknife, to destroy Purplelake. It has cost us more than we have gained by it."

Snakeknife was silent as Warchariot continued, "Let us lie awake and wait for him to come in darkness. Then we will seize him in the dead of night."

But Waterbear climbed into his battle chariot with its scythed wheels and launched a fierce attack that evening on the warcamp of the Hillwolves in a revenge for the murder of the horses.

And a great noise arose, as the demons yelled and ghosts awoke and screamed who had not lived for many hundred years. The Mooncrow laughed like a flying hag. Like a crone of filth she flew overhead and cursed the battle scene. The strife that the devils stirred was loud, hard and ear-piercing. It stabbed the ears like the strike of a sharp arrow. The fiends of war flew over the Waterbear and called on him to kill and slake their thirst for human blood.

The Four Witches of Kill flew high above and hissed and petrified the air with the dead smell. Like the bad breath of lions on the loose or tigers tearing their prey apart. The buzzards circled high even in darkness. Weapons of the warriors cried out in agony to satiate their lusts for broken bones and slaughtered bodies.

Horse servants built a fire. They saw in the fiery flames the faces of Hillwolves. Warchariot and Snakeknife gloated in the flames as keen and deadly as the snapping jaws of crocodiles. All those in the great war camp shook with a trembling running through the blood.

A great fury and rage came on Waterbear as he saw the huge numbers of the Hillwolves with no Wavewarrior to stand beside him. The cold East wind blew fiercely on the fire and through the greenwood trees. It conjured up the faces of vile fiends. They saw the apes of grin, skeletons of the long gone fallen in the battle who had departed many years ago. Those who had died by sword and by the pestilences that always follow after black scenes of death.

And Waterbear stood up in his war chariot, grasping two javelins, his shield and sword. He swung the sword and beat upon his shield until it rang with an ear-spitting din. He whirled his spear, then cried aloud. His yell of killfury shook the blood and trembled the heart. The air demons, death goblins and laughing elves answered his yell with screeching of their own.

The Hillwolf enemy became insane with fear in the slight moonlight. Then confusion seized their weapons in the darkness. They flung themselves in panic and disorder upon the swords and spearpoints of their friends. As chaos reigned they stabbed out at each other, killing their comrades, sons, daughters, wives and sweethearts. Fathers and mothers were the dead of night.

And the buzzards of the sea flew down and smelling the dead bodies of men and women, they gorged themselves and gloated in the blood.

CHAPTER SEVENTEEN
THE GREAT CIRCUIT

Waterbear woke up like a cock at the screech of dawn and strode into his armored chariot. He wore the cloak of speed and shadow vision that came upon him briefly when he killfuried. So swift and furious was his chariot-run that it soon blurred into invisibility. His chariot was drawn by the Great White Stallion and a great black stallion that had been captured when Waterbear had saved his herds from thieves.

The horses wore the mail of iron and gold across their foreheads and their forehand chests. The chariot was studded with sharp knives pointing outwards from pole and yoke and carriage like the scythed wheels that stretched out to the foe. The chariot was like a rolling martial hedgehog with spikes and points bristling and threatening from javelins, knives, swords, spears, lances and daggers.

Waterbear wore a purple silken tunic pinned together with a white broach of pure silver, gold inlaid, like a bright lantern shining on his chest. The thick cloak over his shoulders was many colored, drawn from the cold sea creatures of the ice with skins of black and silver and brown and fawn and white.

He held a copper shield with chains of gold around an orle of red bronze on its rim. His sword was golden hilted, carved with ivory. His spear was lean and lithe with golden rivets.

Then Waterbear called on a charioteer and told him, "I have challenged that great army, a hundred thousand fighting men or more, to send me one man who can stand before me and no one has stepped forward. So I will now ask you to take me on a tour of battle to treat this army as a field of corn and cut it down like harvest in the fall.

Then the charioteer took the whips and goads and crouched over the reins, wearing his armor and mail over a stiff, hard deerskin tunic. He wore sharp studded amulets and steel stud gloves. He reared the two great stallions into a gallop as they snorted great clouds of steam with sparks of fire. Then he drove them towards the Hillwolf battle camp.

The Waterbear stood tall and proud in his chariot. He was dressed in his tunic of stiff waxed bear leather covered in mail of iron tied down with ropes and chains. This was to make sure that it held in place and did not fall apart when Waterbear grew fierce and fiery in his battle fury.

The shield that was chained to his left arm had a sharp edge as keen as any sword. This shield was swung and hurled like any weapon, like any sword or axe or spear ready to slash and cut down foes as a miller grinds the corn. Inside the shield were 20 balanced daggers clipped firmly in the hollow secret part, ready to be taken out and thrown at foes. In his right hand he held the short thick sword that hacked through iron and wood and flesh and bone.

Then the Waterbear grew tense and killfuried. His hair grew thick and white and turned to fur just like his name, the water or polar bear, the king of ice and cold water and snow. Like a bear charging the huntsmen in the forest, he set fire to the chariot's standing platform so that the smoke obscured his swinging sword.

Waterbear wore his ridged and studded steel Helmet of Cry that screamed insults and threats. There the hobgoblins shrieked out in all the agony of dying and with the demons of the battle and the ghosts of battle dead. As warriors of the Hillwolves were cut down by Waterbear's sharp sword and shield, they fell in rows heaped high upon each other's bodies. As the charioteer crouched low behind the horses on his yoketrap, he steered the smoking chariot like a death machine along the rows of dead piled high on either side.

Arms, heads and legs of hound and horse and human, male and female, grinning and twisted, challenged those who passed by. "Guess who I am – this is a masquerade? Guess who this skull belonged to when it lived?" But the piles of bodies brought no answer back. There was no mix and match in that cold morgue and all remained a random mortuary. Death was anonymous in that waxworks show hacked out in pieces by the Waterbear.

A pillar of red hot steam rose up from the neck of Waterbear as he carved out his bloody path among the Hillwolves.

So great was the slaughter that the fieldmarshal of the Hillwolves, Sternrider, the best warrior of Warchariot and Snakeknife, took up his chariot drawn by the Great Bay Stallion. He drove out onto the field to stop the mayhem. But he could not even come anywhere near to Waterbear, so high were the piles of dead stacked up on every side. They were like riverbanks that channeled the flow of blood from Waterbear.

Twice more the chariot of the Waterbear ploughed a wide circuit all around the Hillwolves just to make sure that none of them escaped without having to face his death-machine. Not all the Hillwolves died but all fought hard to stay alive and some lost limbs or eyes.

After this rout, the king Warchariot and his vile queen Snakeknife sent for Sternrider and told him, "Stop this slaughter or we will hold you personally responsible for the war."

Sternrider bowed and told them, "I will fight the Waterbear and stop him, hand-to-hand in combat, face-to-face and man-to-man. How could you doubt me, mighty king and queen? Of course we must take time to rest our warriors from this great onslaught. Just a brief respite for us to catch a breath for combat against the Waterbear, after our hard fighting."

Though it was seen that the Waterbear was tired, wounded and worn out after his great circuit against the Hillwolves, yet Sternrider showed no haste to lead his men against the Waterbear. Meanwhile the hawks flew up and watched the buzzards pick the bones and skulls upon the fields of carnage and mayhem and fierce killfury.

CHAPTER EIGHTEEN
TRUTHTELLER ARRIVES

After his chariot circuit of the Hillwolves, Waterbear drove to his stone island fastness. There he fell into a low and troubled sleep, walking in that steep, moving landscape where the present and the past and future meet. There time is swirling like green hills of seawaves, always undulating and interchanging in madness as the sea moves in confusion and turmoils.

In these wave swinging and treacherous high mountains, the mind and thoughts of Waterbear turned around and shook about like corks in a high tide. He saw the vision of the Great Bay Stallion, the Foresthorse, come prancing and proud flicking his mane and tail and stepping high and challenging to meet the White in mortal combat, face-to-face and horse-to-horse.

The Great White Stallion, Oceanhorse, was flecked with foam and waves, as guardian of the East. The White neighed deeply. Both horses reared up on their strong hind legs and struck their forelegs fiercely at each other. Both pranced and bowed and shook their manes and tails before they snorted and turned around. They galloped back to their herds and rounded them up together and led them forward in stampede towards each other. The Bay's herd was the largest and most powerful. It plunged right through the smaller, weaker herd led by the Great White Stallion. The White's herd became confused and broke up and dispersed as the Bay's herd held together and rolled on.

When Waterbear saw this vision in his sleep he tossed and turned and cried out in despair.

Springvision touched his forehead and spoke quietly, "Be calm, you have been wounded and distressed. You feel that all is lost and that you are alone. I also wonder why our fieldmarshals and all their heroes seem to have deserted. I fear that there is magic in the air, night's visions come to you of flat defeat. Do not believe them, they are lying dreams sent to your mind by the Four Witches of Kill who have been recruited to the Hillwolves side.

"It always has seemed odd to me that all the sad misfortunes of the war have happened to us at such an early stage. The disappearance of Whitehair, then the loss of our four great battalions and their great leaders; the death of Purplelake, the mother of Whitehair, the theft of horses that we will need for war. All these misfortunes are not striking the enemy. Is there a plan, a plot, a strategy behind all this? I wish and pray that we could find the wisdom we need to sieze the key to victory."

Springvision went to the high window and saw the far tents and the war camps of the Hillwolves. But Waterbear, being tired and wounded, lay on his couch and closed his eyes and rested from his wounds.

As Springvision looked and wept over the fields of a hundred thousand Hillwolves in the camps, she cried out, "I can see a lean, tall man. He walks with pride. His eyes look straight ahead. His shoulders are erect, he breathes with ease. No one in all that camp is looking at him. It is as though no one can see him walking. It is as though no man is even aware of him. He pays no heed to anyone, right or left. Rather, he strides as though he walks alone. As he approaches, coming straight towards us through the Hillwolf camps, I can see who it is. It is Truthteller, whom I knew in dreams once long ago in another shadowy life."

At once Truthteller stood in the room before them, tall and wise-faced. There hung beside his belt a sheaf of golden darts of truth. These darts were deadly, never failing to kill when striking at the heart of any liar.

"I am Truthteller, the godfather of the boy Wallwave and it will fall to him, when he is grown, to throw two darts – one dart for Snakeknife, one for the Warchariot. I am come to tell you something of the truth, for now he must be trained and trialed well.

"Now, you must sleep for four days to heal your wounds, your bloody cuts, gashes and weariness. I will leave for your healing in sleep, flowers, ferns and tree leaves for your recovery. I cannot tell your four fieldmarshals to come back and fight but I can paint a picture that makes it clear to them what they are doing.

"Also I tell you, though you have done well and valiantly in making the great circuit to terrorize and cut down all your foes, yet you must learn that wars should not be won, only by dealing death. Pacts and alliances are also needed. You must make good deals and honest and honorable bargains when you can for not all foes are liars and deceivers. Also, the Hillwolves are relieved to know that you are lying sick. They wish you dead.

"So that they will not think you weak or vanquished – for you are not, rather you will be victorious – I will walk through them to my sunny home far in the ocean. In this way, they will see me dressed in your weapons and accoutrements. I will not fight for you for it is wrong that I should take sides in a human war. But I can let them see the truth that you are still alive and waiting to return to raid the Hillwolves as you did before."

Then the Truthteller took the helmet and the weapons and all the accoutrements of battle combat that Waterbear had won on the great circuit. He kissed goodbye to Springvision and held the hand of Waterbear and walked away much as he had come, through all the camping fields of Hillwolves. He was still performing tricks of sword and dirk and javelin, sharp backward jumps and the catching of spears and knives. When the Hillwolves saw him come again, they fled. Some threw their spears and javelins from afar but these fell off and did not touch Truthteller so that the legend grew that Waterbear was indestructible and could not be killed.

When the Truthteller returned to his seacoral home, he carefully constructed a wire cage for birds. Then he caught and locked inside the cage four birds: a cria, a crow, a buzzard and a hawk representing the four battalions of Wavewarriors. He tied outside the cage a snarling dog and sent a drawing of this image to the four fieldmarshals who lived in delusions and false images far in the jungles of the Everyoung.

CHAPTER NINETEEN
STERNRIDER'S DOUBLE DEAL

After the great circuit by Waterbear, Warchariot and Snakeknife set up a council to get advice from their top fieldmarshals: Seaspear, Sternrider and Winterwarrior.

The question was "How do we stop the Waterbear?" Or again, "Which one of you will kill the Wavewarrior king, Waterbear?"

Seaspear cried out, "I know what not to do. Do not kill horses on the Seagull side belonging to the Waterbear, unless you want him to killfury and destroy us. Also, my work is only to build up the seaships on both sides, keep them in shape and train our men in all the arts of sea.

"Our pledge and long-term pact between both sides is that we will never ask your Hillwolf sailors, although under my command at every moment, to war against the Wavewarriors, the Seagulls. We pledge to keep our joint fleet whole and in tact to be ready for self-defense in times of future peace. Also, we will enjoy a strong trade protection from the seathieves who lurk in the dark rocks."

Snakeknife added slyly, "Nevertheless, you have your code of honor that forces you to protect your fighting men and ships from death and danger and destruction."

Seaspear was silent and paused to think of this.

Winterwarrior spoke next, "I am the servant, the deputy of our fieldmarshal Sternrider and I will obey his orders, knowing he will never ask me to do what he would not do first. But if I may make a humble contribution, I think we might try offering the Waterbear supplies of food and fish and gold and silver. Just as the queen has said, he is honor bound to help protect his people from the cold, from all the snows and winds and winter hunger."

"Just so," replied Warchariot. "But first, to make that work we need to wreak more havoc upon the eastern lands."

Sternrider suggested, "I do agree with the Winterwarrior here. We seek supremacy over eastern lands and all their peoples, cities, wealth and homes. I do not want to ride over a graveyard that never has been known to raise good crops. Perhaps if we could make a claim of triumph, even a gesture of formal victory, such as a finger or an ear of Waterbear. This would be enough to turn the tide of war and stir our troops to fighting with more hope."

"Just as easy to kill him as take his ear," sneered Snakeknife, "but we'll take what we can get."

"Very well. We are agreed," said the Sternrider, "I will lead a small crack company against the Waterbear but all my men will be well under my control for help, supplies and carrying weapons. I will fight the bear alone in single combat, man-to-man and face-to-face. When I rout the Waterbear, you should be ready to invade behind me. Is this agreed?"

Yes, all agreed with this. Their worried and fearful faces became brightsmiled as they bowed and shook the hand of Sternrider.

Waterbear slept for four days after the Great Circuit and his wounds were slightly healing with herbs, spices and honeys but he was not quite healed or fit for battle. But Sternrider and Seaspear and the Warchariot were not aware that Waterbear was still unfit for combat. They had seen the Truthteller depart in the disguise of the Waterbear, tall and waractive and performing swordplay, intricate feats of battle, somersaulting and catching daggers in the air.

***

Meanwhile, back at the fortress of Waterbear, Springvision pleaded with her husband, "Do not go today. You are not healed. Give it another month."

But Waterbear replied, "War waits for no one."

And indeed, at that time, Sternrider was preparing to lead a small but deadly company down to the straits, picking a hidden place shaded by rocks from wind and waves and spies.

Later, Waterbear approached fully weaponed for combat to meet with the Sternrider on the field of battle.

Sternrider had told his troops, "Lay back and keep behind me, back me up if necessary if I call on you. Otherwise keep back while I negotiate with Waterbear. For I have known him for many a year in combat."

Sternrider approached the Waterbear with respect, his sword undrawn, his daggers in their scabbards. He motioned to his servants to come forward with a drinking horn of red wine and a plate of silver salmon.

"I wish to talk to you," he told brave Waterbear.

The Waterbear agreed, "Let us be brief. This is no time for wine drinking or feasting."

"Agreed," said Sternrider, "these tokens are only the symbols of respect and honor between us two."

"I do agree," said Waterbear, "In all our dealings I have found you honest and better than honest, honorable and generous."

"I have always tried to be a man of courage in mind as well as body," replied Sternrider. "War is more than piling up refuse dumps of dead bodies. I am the friend as well as the fieldmarshal of your comrade and fellow sailor, Seaspear, fiercest of Seagull warriors. Seaspear and I are well agreed upon our aims of peace and self-protection for both sides in the future."

The Waterbear replied, "You talk of peace but all your acts are stabs of cruel warfare. Your king and queen, Warchariot and Snakeknife, have never offered us a chance of peace."

"You are right, I do agree," replied Sternrider. "And that is why I wish to offer you a pact, a deal between the two of us. I cannot speak for Snakeknife or Warchariot. They are ruthless and rapacious as you say but all men fear them for they seized control of the Hillwolves by deception and illusion.

"They still practice strange arts. Let us ignore them and make a secret bargain between ourselves. Let us be comrades for a future day when Snakeknife and Warchariot will be gone. We should agree that we will never stab our sword against each other. For if we warred in face-to-face, person-to-person combat, we both would surely perish.

"When I raise my sword against you, I will cry in triumph and you will run away. I will not follow."

At this the crias swooped and yelled in anger.

Sternrider continued, "I will not storm your fastness. You will live under my guarantee of peace and safety until you gather together your great armies and move against Warchariot and Snakeknife. This should not be seen as empty theatre or they might overrule my treaty terms. I do believe that they would burn you out. Naturally, I must invade the inland horsemoor regions of your land. You can be sure that I will never kill your horses – that was cruelty. Nor will I move against your harbors or your fleet of ships. For who knows when your four fieldmarshals will return with all their crack divisions?"

"I cannot do this, Sternrider," said the Waterbear. "You need to know that in all my life I have never fled before a foe in any war with sea pirates or thieves. I am known as a champion who never fled from a foe. I cannot do this. Rather, I would give you anything but this. However, I believe that this would be the right time for me to do a deal for amnesty."

"Look, Waterbear, this pact is not a deal – it is a double deal, for I will do the same for you. You will draw your sword and yell 'Retreat' and I will flee with all my men when one day we will meet in the final battle. You are well known as a hero who is fearless but the first task of a champion is to win. Retreat before me now and, in return, I will flee before you when the last fight roars around us. You owe it to your men to make this pact."

Then Waterbear remembered the wise words of Truthteller who said, 'Wars are not won only by dealing death but also by alliances and pacts and armistices.' Also, Waterbear remembered he was tired and weakened by the force of the Great Circuit, though the Sternrider knew nothing of this.

He snapped his sword more tightly in its sheath and bowed and shook the hand of Sternrider, "Your offer promises a lot for little. I will expect to see you on the day of final reckoning for that last day will surely come and I will claim the victory."

Sternrider shook the hand of Waterbear and briefly bowed, "This pact will bring me trouble on that last day but better then than now and I have been in trouble many times before and I have always found escape. You have my word and bond that I will lead the last retreat as I have promised you."

Sternrider drew his sword and yelled, "Retreat." Then the Waterbear climbed into his chariot and fled before Fieldmarshal Sternrider and fortified himself and Queen Springvision and all their servants and accoutrements of war and all their longboats in their harbor.

Sternrider left them on their island castle and swept his armies past their harbor fastness into the high horsemoors and village homes of the farms and fields and blacksmiths of the East.

When he returned to the Hillwolf camp he came before King Warchariot and Snakeknife who were in a conference with Seaspear and the Winterwarrior.

Sternrider bowed before this council of Hillwolves and humbly presented to them his claim of victory. "The Bear has fled before me and is hiding upon his island fastness. We can rule in all the high lands, farms and fields and moors. In all parts of the East where Waterbear no longer rules, where I have freed the land. We have won a nominal victory today. Of course, we can find another warrior, one of us here, to go into his fastness and root him out and kill him."

No one spoke until the Snakeknife sneered, "Go back yourself – you said that you would kill him. Keep your word."

"That is not true. I said that I would rout him and so I did and not one man among you, nor among all these armies, has defeated him."

Warchariot was suspicious of Sternrider. "Remember he who fights and runs away will live to fight again some other day. I do not want his flight," said Warchariot, "I want his head."

The Sternrider replied, "Within my hand I grasped the rock of the East. I claim this land in the name of Warchariot. Now and forever that land will be yours and all the machines of war and warriors that live there. We will rule earth, fire, wind and water, both animals and humans will be yours."

Warchariot replied, "All this is very formal."

"You have the claim in law for all his lands," said Sternrider.

But Warchariot insisted once again, "I do not want his claim. What do I care for law? I am the law. Go back and get his head."

Seaspear spoke to the king, "You said that you would take what you could get from Waterbear – you have the victory. Let that be enough."

Then Winterwarrior agreed, "A win is everything."

But the Snakeknife persisted, "You must go back and finish him. It will be easy now that he has been defeated. He is sick and wounded, weak at the knees no doubt after his turmoils."

Sternrider spoke, "My final word is this. No one but me has put the Waterbear to flight. Of all our heroes who have died trying, no warrior has defeated him and no one else but me has even come close. I will not go even one more time to fight the Waterbear, I swear, until my turn comes round again."

CHAPTER TWENTY
WATERBEAR'S EXILE

The Waterbear returned to his stone fastness and called together his servants and near family to tell them, "We must go to visit Wallwave, Stormbolt and Shadowhero, far away on the remote islands where they live. There we must wait until I have recovered and can take up again the axe of war, for though the Hillwolves do not know that I am badly wounded, they think I am laid low, at least for now. They will be devastating parts of the East that are located far from the harbors."

Springvision wore her sword and shield and armor, her cloak of mail and helmet of full warning. This helmet screamed aloud when danger lurked nearby. She wore all the accoutrements of a warriorwoman, dirks and knives with iron balls loosely swinging upon her wrists, ready to strike the foe.

Springvision rode in the first chariot with the scythed wheels rolling. She scanned the roads ahead, for the Hillwolves were marauding here and there.

When the Waterbear and Springvision arrived at the home of Shadowhero, Waterbear took himself aside to a quiet chamber where he could recover from his wounds and rest after the hardships of the long journey.

Springvision spoke to both her young sons and told them of the war that was brewing and of the Great Circuit that had left their father Waterbear wounded and sick. "However, the Waterbear will soon be well recovered from his tiredness and his sickness. Then he will go again against the Hillwolves. However, you cannot yet join in the attack for every champion of the Wavewarriors must first be trained in the three types of skill to become ready for every situation."

And Springvision spoke to her two sons about the arts of warfare to persuade them not to seek battle combats until their skills had been well tried and tested and matured, for they were known to strain at the leash of training.

"The first skill is to handle weapons well – swords, spears and axes, talking spears and helmets, javelins and throwing knives or dirks and daggers. The mighty axes that require great strength. The coats of mail and armor for the neck, the chest and thighs, leaving no door unguarded. There are the knee and wrist strengtheners and swinging irons to strike into the face of the enemy when he breaks down your sword or spear in combat. And you must know the tricks, the turns, the leaps, the somersaults for handling these accoutrements of war.

"The next skill that you need is the skill of work - the knowledge and wisdom of a long experience with all the uses of small arms. These skills result from finding the same fighting combinations.

"Perhaps you will experience a sling shot or an arrow bolt to strike from afar off, then a javelin throw. Also, this may be followed by a close encounter with a sword or spear or daggers – then you remember from previous days the long, the short or close-up and you are ready for the same routines to follow in the same way.

"Then you need the opposite – the wit to deal with modes of murder and treachery that you have never seen or known before. For example, a huge army surrounds you or the ground opens when you are sleeping or the ceiling springs a dark and quiet assassin when you sit eating and unaware and you have heard only a rustle to warn you from the roof.

"How do you deal with these wit-testing thrusts when neither knowledge nor experience teaches – only originality will help you after you have been tried and tested well with cunning and treachery, time and again."

"Nevertheless my Mother, training must end," replied the boy Wallwave, "Real life must start someday and I am nearly finished now."

Shadowhero nodded, "I will tell you when you have completed the training of a warlord and if our heroes and fieldmarshals return then I will let you join them under their guidance."

***

Meanwhile the armies of the Sternrider swept into the remote parts of the East, avoiding the coastal fringes where the harbors lay, as the Fieldmarshal Sternrider had promised.

However, Queen Snakeknife had her own secret plans and ordered the sub-commanders under the rank of fieldmarshal to seek out signs of seamen. They were to look for symbols or ships or parts of boats and chariots or fishing nets or harpoons or the like. For not all seamen live nearby the harbors. They should put the seamen clans to death at once to make sure they could never use their boats to strike against the Hillwolves in the future.

This was despite the best peace efforts of Seaspear, the overall fieldmarshal of both fleets. For Seaspear failed to keep his trust and promise that all his seamen would be well protected from the cruel ravages and winds of war.

The Hillwolves slashed and cut both farms and homes, burning the barns and food stores to the ground. And old men, retired and resting from their many years of battle, sighed and shook their heads in shame, looking upon the ashes of their homes. Watching the kidnapping of their young grandchildren they muttered bitterly among themselves, "What have we now to lose but our old bones? Why did we never have good luck and prosper?

"Perhaps it was to snare us for this day? Soon we will be destroyed. Food for the buzzards. See how they gather and swoop from skies above – they smell the stench of death before we die. Let us drink up our youth in this strong potion – if any youth is left in empty bottles. Let us throw one last stab at these Hillwolves. And even if we should be cut to pieces, we can raise the cost of conquest by a few limbs."

Another rabblerouser spoke, "Let us first hide away the Great White Stallion and his small herd of war horses. We know where they are stamping on the nearby moors. Now we can take them to the secret caves against the day when our young men return."

And this was done. Then the old men climbed aboard the creaking chariots with their rusty swords and their broken shields and scabbards. Clutching their javelins and blunt old swords, they flung themselves upon the wolf invaders. Like ghosts returning to their past scenes of battle, these sad men were like a legion from the tombs, with the Grim Reaper leading the charge against a startled foe who never expected to die before these former heroes.

On that day, the old Seagull heroes slaughtered many more than three times their own number before they fell upon the sands of combat.

But when Warchariot came upon the scene of battle and saw his slaughtered Hillwolf warriors lying around like food for crows and buzzards, he and Snakeknife called for the Sternrider. "Send us Seaspear," they told their wise fieldmarshal.

CHAPTER TWENTY ONE
COMBAT OF THE RED HAND

In the dead of night Sternrider came to visit the Waterbear to tell him to expect the great Wavewarrior Seaspear in single combat. Along with the Sternrider was Gentleleaf, the Queen of Seaspear, who had come to visit Springvision.

Waterbear cried, "But Seaspear is my friend, my fellow fighter in the pirate wars, my former comrade in the battle.

"Nevertheless, Warchariot and Queen Snakeknife have now persuaded the brave Seaspear to stand and fight against you. Seaspear is bound in honor to protect the seamen of his fleets. Snakeknife has pointed out to the Seaspear that day-by-day there are many seamen dying as long as you keep the great war alive. Not all seamen live near the harbors. Some have died inland and she tells Seaspear he has abandoned those who trusted him – like the dead Queen of Justice. Seaspear is sad and broken but he sees no other way to clear his name and honor."

But Springvision replied, "We all implored him not to ally with Warchariot and Snakeknife, even to protect his seamen and his fleet. There is no such thing as an honorable war. War is the place where truth and honor die with split alliances and hollow promises. Only the buzzards rule and reign victorious. Everything else: homes, ships, farmfields – perish. There is no honor in war – only black cinder and yet wars must be fought as best we can to save just rule from unjust boots and bayonets."

Then Gentleleaf, the loyal Queen of Seaspear, pleaded with Waterbear, "Do not go out – for if the two great warriors of the Seagulls should ever combat, one of you must die."

Waterbear replied, "I have run away one time already. If I did so twice I would lose my kingdom first and then my head. It is impossible. You must tell Seaspear that he can join us fully and abandon Snakeknife and Warchariot."

Gentleleaf wept, "I have begged and pleaded with Seaspear to do so but he is adamant that he must kill you and so avenge his honor. This is war, no one can stand with one foot on each side."

Then Sternrider shook hands with Waterbear, climbed back into his chariot and left. Gentleleaf also climbed into her chariot and drove off alongside the Sternrider. However, when they returned to the camp of the Hillwolves they received side glances of suspicion.

Then Seaspear moved his camp to the great straits and told his servants to lay out his arms and all his old accoutrements of war, including his sheaf of javelins and dirks. They did so in silence and in sorrow for they were Seagulls. They knew that they would lose one of their champions of war because of the machinations of Snakeknife.

Soon the Waterbear was visited by Seaspear. And Waterbear greeted him with words of their past friendship. "My dear friend, welcome. This is like days past."

They drank the red wine of old times together and ate the venisons of battle courage.

Then Waterbear reminisced, "War is a greedy witch – we call her Mooncrow – she flies at night and caws and calls for food. She cries for more and more food and drink and servile slavery. Neverending is her greed. If only we could break off from her clutches and, once we had escaped, we could be free to build and sow good food for health and growth and strength. But while the greedy witch clings to our backs we can do nothing but to heed and feed her. Her war demands are endlessly bloodgreedy. Here's to the death of the greedy witch Mooncrow. Here's to the death of greed insatiate."

Then the two heroes drank a small toast to the demise of war and all her death-fiends and demands.

"Before the warwitch took over the world, life was relaxed and rested in the sunshade with a clear glass of afternoon white wine." And the Waterbear continued thoughtfully, "Let us look forward to those days again when the only shadows on our long pavilions were skirmishes and petty fights with pirates. There we fought side-by-side and helped each other."

After a small supper they went their separate ways to rest. That night their horses stood together in the same paddock. All their servants sat at the same fire. And when the heroes went their homeward ways they kissed like brethren who had long been lost and separate from each other.

Next morning at the screech of dawn the heroes arose like fighting cocks, strutting and crowing, happy to be alive and fit to fight. They bowed and raised their swords and saluted each other from their two camps. Each camp was on the other shore beside the swirling waters of the straits. They came together in the western camp and drank the clear stream water of wakefulness. They picked the bones of pigeons roasted on spits, then they once more embraced like brothers and took their separate places on each side of the narrow straits. The waters swirled between the rocky shores - but shallowly and reluctantly they swirled.

That day, the Waterbear shot many slingstones. But Seaspear avoided every shot by taking cover behind his shield or by leaping well clear of all the flying missiles. Likewise the Waterbear avoided all the arrows and small knives shot out by Seaspear.

Then Waterbear shot javelins and dirks at Seaspear who shot throwing-knives and spears back at the Waterbear – but all shots missed as Waterbear jumped high and leapt away. These light missiles flew back and forth like butterflies on a warm, breezy, sunlit day in spring. Flies, bees and wasps were buzzing and zipping around and neither hero scored a hit with anything. They both tried hard to end the struggle quickly with a lucky bloodless strike that left one champion stunned and deep-sleeping rather than cold and dead.

They hoped that one of the heroes would suffer from loss of blood or breath. But there was no such sudden break in combat. So both heroes fought with airborne missiles until nightfall clouded their flying weapons.

Then both fell on each other, neck on neck, in the longtime brotherhood of old comrades. They laid down to rest at their own fires for they were weary of the flying weapons.

They both exchanged their red wine and their venison, their healing herbs and potions for recovery, roasted over their fires and shared together. They sent their drinks and venison to each other, sharing like brothers-in-arms in a joint remembrance of war for oldtimes sake.

That night their horses stood in the same paddock and all their servants sat at the same fire until the morning light.

Then, once again, at the screech of dawn, the heroes arose like fighting cocks, crowing and strutting, happy to be alive and fierce to fight. They bowed and raised their swords and saluted each other from their two camps, each on the other shore beside the swirling waters of the straits. Again they joined together in the West camp and drank the pure stream water of wakefulness. Picking the bones of pigeons roasted on spits, they once more embraced and kissed like brothers. Then they took their separate places in their chariots both drawn by powerful stallions and held broadswords in hand, axes and spear-lances.

They both were dressed in all the accoutrements of combat: helmets and mail and chains and body armor and both drove hard at each other in the straits. They hacked and hewed and slashed and cut and swung until the water in the straits turned red.

All the long day they gashed and tore and wounded each other but neither one achieved a fatal blow until they wearied as the shadows fell.

Then they passed over their weapons to their servants and fell upon each other, neck on neck, in the longtime brotherhood of old comrades.

They laid down to rest at their own fires and both exchanged their white wine and their boarmeat roasted over their fires on two long spits. They also exchanged their healing potions and their healthy herbs, sharing like brothers-in-arms in a joint remembrance of old campaigns.

That night their horses slept in the same stable and their servants watched at the same fire, until the morning light.

When the third day of combat brightened in the East, at the first screech of dawn, Waterbear rose up like a fighting cock still stretching his wings, happy to be alive and ready to fight.

As he drew near to the straits he saw there was no sharing or greeting from Seaspear. Rather, he seemed withdrawn, silent and brooding within himself, alone with his own thoughts. His posture was stooped over and his steps unsure.

Noting these things, the Waterbear was seized with a great sadness and sympathy for Seaspear and he said, "Remember our old friendship and the days when we both fought on the same side like comrades. Let that friendship still flourish till we reach old age and sit in quiet contemplation. I pray you, Seaspear, walk away from this and sail your ships among the Wavewarriors. Your honor is now satisfied since you have hard fought for two days against me here – no other warrior has ever done so . . ."

But Seaspear shook his head, still stunned and glassy, "It is too late to walk away, we must fight to the death, then one of us may walk when honor has been settled."

And Seaspear called for his extra body armor and skins, his plates of iron as protection against the Bonespear. This was the spear that thirsted for human blood and never failed to find it. This spear was found along the shores of the sea after a storm. It had been formed by wind out of the bones of heroes killed in the storms. Such was its thirst for blood that the Bonespear had to be soaked in red wine daily.

When Waterbear heard Seaspear ask for this armor, he told his servants, "Hold the Bonespear ready for me to use, if ever I should ask for it as a last resort."

Then Waterbear returned to the eastern side in his chariot. He waited solemnly for Seaspear to get ready for the combat on the western shore. Seaspear wore thick skins hardened by tanning, a plate of iron chained over the skins as an extra armament. Seaspear urged his small charioteer to sit well forward between the horses while he drove fierce as a storm towards Waterbear.

Then likewise, Waterbear urged his chariot forward and both sides clashed together in the strait, parting the low ebb waters in the middle so that the foam flew high into the air and the rocky bottom of the sea lay clear. Both heroes rained great blows upon each other with axe and hammer and broadsword and spear. The demons of the weapons screamed in hatred – even their shields were battered into scrap. But neither won the victory. Blow on blow fell hard upon each other. It was as though the blows fell on a body hard as rock – a heart of stone against a heart of ice.

At last the quivering javelin of Seaspear found a small crack in the armor of the Waterbear - a slit to let in death. It struck. The blood flowed from the wound like a thin river that colored red the flowing tide of sea.

As Waterbear was weakened, he cried out in desperation, "Throw me the Bonespear now."

As Waterbear caught the Bonespear in the air. He turned it round and drove it through the body of Seaspear as he stood upon his chariot. The Bonespear, made from the dead bodies of heroes, forged in the storms of sea, could never fail. It drove through all the layers of hide and chain and iron plates and sank deep into Seaspear as it reached out greedily for the blood of champions.

Then Seaspear gasped and sank upon his knees. Feeling the Bonespear eat into his heart and thirstily drink his blood, he cried to Waterbear, "Comrade the pain is over – it is the end." And Seaspear lay back on the rocks and spoke, "Lend me your sword, friend Waterbear, one last time."

Waterbear turned the sharp blade of his sword towards his own heart, in an unspoken invitation that said, 'Let us both die at once, for war is futile.' He offered the sword hilt to Seaspear, who smiled and shook his head, "The way is long and hard – not short and easy." Seaspear grasped hard on the hilt of the broadsword of Waterbear. Seaspear leaned on one elbow. He swung the sword and cut off his left hand. Seizing the bloody hand, he threw it far onto the eastern shore and said, "That's where my heart and hand will live forever, at least in the remembrance of my combat."

Waterbear shook his head, "That was not needed. I gladly would have carried you to that shore."

And Waterbear, despite his deep and painful javelin wound, lifted up his comrade Seaspear and carried him. He laid him on the eastern shore where he would sleep with all his fellow Wavewarriors and not on the western shore with cunning Hillwolves. And Waterbear left his comrade gently sleeping beside his red and severed cold left hand.

CHAPTER TWENTY TWO
MARCHES OF WAR

Then a gloom, a sigh of despair fell upon the Seagulls as once again their king, Waterbear, was wounded. And Gentleleaf went to the side of the slain Seaspear and mourned for him and placed him in her chariot to take him to the castle of Waterbear. There she set him up in his accoutrements of war and armor, mail and helmet, sword, shield and weapons and then placed him upon the prow of his best warship.

The ship was set on fire and steered West to sail to the Islands of the Everyoung, there to be mourned by the weeping breezes from the East, with howls from the ghosts of long-gone drowned sailors. And hawks flew up around the burial ship to represent the past triumphs of Seaspear.

Queen Gentleleaf lamented, "He was a pillar of peace and quiet stability and yet a lion for fierceness when he stood against the foe. He was a dragon from the waves of turmoil. Seamen and brave Wavewarriors served him and paid him homage, for they trusted him. He was a fieldmarshal who loved his men but treachery and cunning machinations trapped him in the dread grip of honor that destroys. My sight has gone from me since I first saw you lying alone and slain upon the shore of victory beside the bloody hand of war – the war that leads only to death. He was a wave of wild winds, unstoppable. Yesterday he was a mountain, but today he is a ghost howling among the sea breezes of dead sailors. There is no life for me after this loss. There is no vengeance more for me to find – Seaspear was the victim of his honor – I have no love for any man alive. My life can only bring me pain and sorrow."

Then Gentleleaf put her mouth to Seaspear's mouth and put her arms around his neck and sailed far into the western ocean on the ship that glowed and crackled in the pale sunset.

As the Wavewarriors fell into despair for lack of hope, they thought of their fieldmarshals – the four fieldmarshals of their four divisions – the Stormleaper of the Sea Battalion, Whaleroarer of the Hills and Crags Battalion, the Icedragon, commander of the Plains and Bush Division and Summersailor of the Air and Sky.

And all began to dream and wonder why the box with Crias, Crows, Buzzards and Hawks inside, trapped by a snarling dog, had never given a message to their leaders. This symbol had been made by the Truthteller to tell the four fieldmarshals that they had been lured away from their great army and trapped within a box of dream delusion. The snarling dog represented the four witches who had designed the trap. This picture had never seemed to become clear to the fieldmarshals.

The remnants of the army of Waterbear asked Springvision, "Surely this is clear. The main parts of our army are held captive by mind manipulation and illusion caused by the witches hired by the Hillwolves."

Springvision, like her young niece, Whitehair, had discernment of spirits and understanding of dark dreams. So the Queen Springvision took herself apart and prayed for wisdom to help advise the Seagulls. After some hours she came back to their presence.

"Truthteller will never force his images or messengers upon the life of man. His wisdom is like food upon a coldboard – all may select or not – just as they please. There is a pathway of the mind laid out for all to use if they so wish, it is known as the landscape of visions and dreams. There, any mind may walk to visit another outside the barriers of time and space. I will try it when I sleep and so may you."

But many shook their heads. "We would not try it. We can't take control of our dreams and visions. We always forget our dreams when we wake up."

"Nevertheless," the queen Springvision replied "we must send the message of the Truthteller to our four fieldmarshals in the land of the Everyoung."

***

After a night of deep sleep, the four fieldmarshals in the isles of dreams awoke the next day to realize that they and all their followers and champions had been deceived. They had been lured away by visions of beauty and easy living in the jungles. And they were angry that they had been fooled and deluded into leaving the Seagulls helpless with all their ships, harbors, farmlands and treasures without the benefit of Wavewarrior heroes.

At once they ordered their heroes and champions to seize their arms and all their accoutrements of war and to make ready the warships and prepare to sail.

And the four fieldmarshals of the Wavewarriors drank the white wine of clear vision and ate the salmon of wisdom when they saw the cage of crias, crows, buzzards and hawks, hemmed in by the fierce barking of a wolf-like dog.

And the Seamaster, one of the immortals, shook his green cloak between the Isles of the Everyoung, with their warm jungle trees and the fortified harbors of the Wavewarriors, so that they would forget their long exile.

Tear was the companion of Stormleaper in the Isles of the Everyoung in fountains of rainbows. She was the daughter of fire still burning bright in all her beauty and display of gems.

And Stormleaper came to Tear and said, "As you will know, there are times in the night when dreams rise up before me in dim vision – scenes of the times of old, so I must go."

And Whaleroarer came to Sigh and bid farewell, "I am a warrior and I would be a coward if I remained here, when I should be fighting."

So Sigh gave to Whaleroarer a strong drink of forgetfulness so that he would never hold any memory of Sigh or her true love. Then she said to Whaleroarer, "This drink will set you free for ever. Truly men seek for what they do not have. And what they have seems less than nothing to them."

And Icedragon also said goodbye and sailed from Smile and the Seamaster shook his cloak between them so that they would never meet again.

Then Summersailor came to Laugh and told her, "I need to wage a war as a fieldmarshal. I must sail on the tide."

But Laugh replied, "I am also a warriorwoman, trained and skilled. I will come with you and help you to fight the battle that has subtler plots and plans."

And Summersailor agreed and they sailed away. Yet he remembered nothing of the Isles of the Everyoung nor all its teaming jungles.

***

And Waterbear sat upon his throne above the waves and waters around his stone-built fastness, taking the air and sun high on the ramparts. He was recovering from the stomach wound that had been inflicted by Seaspear before he died.

Following the clear dreamcalls of Springvision, brave Waterbear stood by prepared to watch his fieldmarshals and skippers and all their heroes sail into his harbors. Springvision was well pleased and stood nearby.

CHAPTER TWENTY THREE
THE FIELDMARSHALS RETURN

When the four fieldmarshals sailed for home, there traveled with them all their bodyguards and all their four divisions of the battle. The four divisions were the crias for the sea, the crows to scale the hills and craggy peaks, the buzzards of the bush and dried-up plains to clear the fields of enemy dead bones and the hawks to triumph with their moving troops from one part of the battlefield to another. All sailed in full battalions, fleet on fleet in battleboat or longboat on the waves.

Soon the Four Witches of Kill heard of the sailings and warned King Warchariot and the Snakeknife that Whitehair, as a hostage, was secured and surrounded deep in the witches castle.

"Let them march on you and she will be lost. One of the witches brains will be transplanted and the boy Wallwave will have lost his bride. See that the Waterbear will be forewarned and makes no move to jeopardize her life."

***

Springvision looked to the sea and told Waterbear, "The first time that I surveyed the heroes who were returning home, I saw that all the small animals had left the plains and shrubberies and bushes and taken to the hills.

"The second time I saw a thick sea mist float from the ocean so that it made the tops of hills seem to be islands poking out of a lake of mist and fog. Then I saw sparks of fire in this great mist crackling and flaming and flaring from the sea. Then I saw lightning and heard thunder claps and rending and tearing as of sheets of sail and felt a fierce wind blowing from the sea that almost blew me over the side of the rampart."

And Waterbear replied, "Those are the battalions of the four fieldmarshals who have returned by boat and caused the animals to flee to high ground. The thick sea mist that floated in from sea was the hot breath of the warriors, keen for combat. This was the fog that made the hills seem like islands. The lightnings and the thunders and the flames was the flashing of the fierce eyes of the warriors.

"The clattering of the swords and spears and javelins, the creaking of the chariots, tearing of sails, fury and fierceness and the shouting of the warriors as they tore their tents and slashed the tent walls to reach the enemy. They did not take the time to go through the tent openings and hatches as they strained forward in desire for battle. The claps of thunder were the pounding and neighing of two huge horses pulling Stormleaper's chariot, proud-chested and high-headed. Stormleaper rides his chariot four-square, purple-faced and stocky. He carries a broadsword, heavy and razor sharp at his left side. Is this the man you see?"

"It is," Springvision answered, "and I see also a tall, lean, blond man with a three-pronged spear driving a chariot with two dappled gray horses, strong, swift in battle with great power but ready to stop or turn around at a moment's notice. This man has an aura of deadly and sinister terror."

"This is Icedragon," said the Waterbear, "A man of menace who is swift and sharp."

"Emerging through the mist I see a chariot bedecked with gold and silver and clearly belonging to a strong fieldmarshal," continued Springvision. "Inside the chariot, towering high above the horses, is a giant of a man – a man and a half – with a deep booming voice. He urges on his horses and chief champions and warriors. He waves a heavy broadsword and swings it as though he practices the art of beheading so eager he is for the fight. His voice roars out in fiery threats – 'I'll kill and take your head.' His whole body and chariot and horses throbs with the thrill of bonelust craving death. Who is this giant, screaming for limbs and heads? Who is this war-machine in one great warrior?"

And Waterbear replied, "That is the Whaleroarer, trembling and transformed by a killfury, into chill berserking. The enemy will never stand before him."

Springvision looked again into the armies to see if she could discern the fourth fieldmarshal.

"I see a strong fieldmarshal's chariot bedecked with diamonds and gemstones and bronze but the proud man who stands within its cage is not alone. He bears upon his arm a chain of hawks ready to fly away and lead him to the foe. Also beside him there stands a warriorwoman dressed for battle in helmet, mask and mail and armor plate. Her hair flows freely, she will surely lose it in the affray of battle. Who is she?"

The warrior is the Summersailor. The warriorwoman by his side is Laugh from the Isles of Youth – whoever takes her locks will pay for it with his own locks and head."

CHAPTER TWENTY FOUR

RETURN OF THE BOY WALLWAVE

Then Sternrider sent a message to the Waterbear, "Let us have a time of truce and armistice before you advance your troops against the Hillwolves. Queen Snakeknife, King Warchariot and the Four Witches of Kill now hold your niece as hostage. They may destroy her either in body or in mind or both, if they so wish."

So Waterbear asked Springvision to judge and she replied, "Hold back our troops just now but let the boy Wallwave lead a small party to rescue Whitehair. This will not disturb the Four Witches of Kill, for they will not see this as an overwhelming threat upon them. But yet the boy Wallwave is just finishing his training as a warrior and Whitehair has been promised to Wallwave as his queen. And let us not forget that the boy Wallwave holds in his hands the magic power of waves. Who knows what magic powers he can unleash? Thus we may be able to make a small strike upon them without arousing their full fear and vengeance."

And Waterbear sent back word to the Sternrider, "Thanks for the warning. I will hold my army but the boy Wallwave has been promised Whitehair. I have ruled that only he can rescue her from where she lies in chains in the witches castle."

***

Then the boy Wallwave and his brother Stormbolt, with a few stalwart Wavewarriors for self-protection, stormed on the mighty army of the Hillwolves but made no impact. They were scorned and laughed at like a swarm of bees against a rock-built wall.

Outside the domed dungeon of the witches, the rescue party rested and observed the solid castle steeped in arms and magic. They pointed their spears and swords towards the windows and towards the castle doors and drawbridges.

Inside the castle of the Four Vile Witches, Whitehair lay stretched out on the couch beside a great roaring fire that lit the palace and where the smoke drifted up through the open skylight. She was bound both hand and foot. Her mouth was gagged but her eyes were watching upwards. She groaned and shook her head and she looked up as the fire and flames swirled up and roared beside her. She saw the boy Wallwave among the flames. His face was at the smokehole cut in the round-domed castle of the witches.

The witches gleed and chortled at the sight. The boy Wallwave was always beautiful but more beautiful he seemed at that bright moment when he appeared to Whitehair in the roof. A stunned, short silence fell upon the Hillwolf army as muttering and confusion came upon them.

Then the boy Wallwave flew down through the smoke. He landed just beside Whitehair, seizing her. He put her underneath his strong left arm and taking shield and weapon in his right hand he jumped and flew up through the smoke and sparks, carrying her through the smokehole of the dome. He flew far over the sea to the castle of the Waterbear. For he had special powers as the Wallwave over the earth and fire and air and waters.

A great uproar went up from the Hillwolf army, who had expected only a ground attack. Only a few futile knives had been thrown at the boy Wallwave and his queen.

Stormbolt and his small rescue party looked up and saw Wallwave and Whitehair change in the air into the form of swans. They stretched their wings and necks and flew away, two yellow swans into the red sunset.

Now that Whitehair had been rescued and was no longer a hostage, the armies of the Wavewarriors were set free to throw themselves upon the Hillwolves. Then clash fell upon clash and weaponthunder as the demons of the swords and spears of the Seagulls screamed out for murder, bones and fierce revenge.

But the king, Warchariot, rose and rallied his troops and steadied them with captains and wild threats, telling the captains, "Hold your broadswords ready not for the foe but for your men who weaken. If I see any captain who has not killed, for cowardice, at least one of our own men, I swear I will kill that captain on the spot, cutting his head off like freshcaught fish.

So the Hillwolves fought hard against the Seagulls.

CHAPTER TWENTY FIVE
THE FLIGHT OF THE WOLF

The two sides fought like an entangled forest. Neither side was fit to gain the victory. Then the Waterbear and the Sternrider came face to face, as they had done before.

And brave Waterbear remembered the Truthteller and his advice to make a deal for victory with any one of the enemy who was honorable. Then the vision and the memory of Sternrider rose before him and Waterbear repeated the grim words that Sternrider had promised when they had made a deal, 'Retreat before me now and I will flee before you when the last fight roars around us.'

"So let this be so and flee from me and my Wavewarriors will not pursue your Hillwolves. But rather we will let you all escape, at least the keen swords of turmoil and vengeance."

And Sternrider turned and fled and called on his warriors to help escape the cruel yoke of Warchariot and flee to a safe place. "Come let us move aside and give the field to Waterbear to fight the treacherous killers that your King Warchariot calls captains."

And the forces of the Wavewarriors swept through as the Hillwolves lines broke. Only the Warchariot and his heroes fought a dogged losing battle. But the Sternrider set apart his battalions on an island off the south side of the west bank and held it, surrounded by his champions and heroes, as strong as any fastness in the world. And there they held the Great Bay Stallion, much to the grievance of Queen Snakeknife.

And the Wavewarriors of the Waterbear surrounded but did not invade the Sternrider's island. Soon the Wavewarriors claimed the victory and rode their chariots back with spoils of battle. They captured chariots, horses and servants along with musical instruments, helmets, swords and axes, javelins, carpets, silks and fabrics, chains of mail, jewels and gems, plates and cups of gold and silver, books of tales and songs.

The Hillwolves crept impoverished into the woods, the crevasses and caverns of the shadowlands. Like hawks arising over the battlefield was the victory of the Waterbear and his Wavewarriors over the King Warchariot and his poisonous assassin Queen Snakeknife. For these two lurked in holes and watercaves to plot and plan revenge on the Sternrider. For it was clear that Sternrider had helped the Waterbear in his attack on Hillwolves.

At first Snakeknife and Warchariot laid low, hiding in their remote fastness but later they sought the plots of the Four Witches of Kill.

CHAPTER TWENTY SIX
THE FALL OF THE WOLF

The witches worked in secret, far from Waterbear and his protection of the exiled Hillwolves who had changed sides and fought alongside the Sternrider. The Four Witches of Kill gathered around and agreed to use their spells and strange aromas of mindmadness and deceptions and delusions drawn from the very pit of demons and distractions.

Meteoreyes said to the other Witches of Kill, "Mindmadness is the ruse that clouds the reason. This is our best illogic of persuasion. But first we need a weapon fit for death that we can use to overwhelm the Sternrider. Sternrider has now changed allegiances and fights for Waterbear. We must destroy our new-found enemy. Let us sharpen and make keen our deadliest poison smeared on the knives and swords and javelins so that the slightest scratch or even touch from the sharp edges will bring instant death."

Then they called on every wisp of leaves and straw and grass and twigs and flowers dying and dead that flew about in the autumn ground and sky. They cried aloud, "Take on the shape of a huge invading army of men and boats floating in from sea upon the waves of a white-foam topped wallwave."

It seemed to Sternrider that it was about to overwhelm and swallow up the floating, straggling flotsam of small victims even on a calm and waveless sunny day. This vision of a great invading army filled all the landscape with fierce shouting and yelling as smoke and fire burnt on and crackled brightly. The leaves and grass flew up like screaming devils appearing to surround Sternrider like a sea of hideous, armed, laughing deathhead foes.

The friends of Sternrider tried to steady him, telling him, "Do not panic. Do not be afraid of these dark fiends. These shadows cannot harm you. They are the grasses and the leaves of autumn that dance and dangle in the winds and whirlwinds. The sounds you hear are hums and whines of breezes, all made to sound and seem like threats and weapons. These are not the fierce howls of warfiends and vile assassins but rather they are the threatening armies raised up in hell only to lure you to mindmadness and fear. These false spells and malvisions are not real."

Waterbear heard of Sternrider's illness and mindmadness and delusions from the Witches of Kill. So he sent his best musicians and taletellers to Sternrider to play upon the harp and sing the songs of sunlit summer days - to drive away the threats of noise and turmoil.

Warchariot and Snakeknife crept to the island of their defeated fieldmarshal as the four witches continued the attack from the whipped leaves and grasses of the wind. They made them scream like hoards of warriors. And Windweasal appeared before Sternrider like a warriorwoman of the storm. Meteoreyes took the form of a charioteer whose chariot burnt up and cindered all its deadly weapons.

As the Sternrider fled from the strange sight, he saw Rivershark appear as a young woman washing her snow-white linen in a river and as she washed the linen, it turned red and sent great floods of blood flowing away. A voice said, "This is Washerwoman, for you she washes the fresh linen that turns red and flows away like blood – this is your fate."

Landslink rose up as a ghost from the dark grave and cried, "I come from deep beneath the earth where you are buried in a pit. No eyes, no brain, no smell, no taste, no feeling, no existence is your fate in this dark grave."

Sternrider was now frozen in dismay and Warchariot seized the deadly poisoned spear and threw it at his late fieldmarshal's chest. At once the poison spread around his veins and the once strong fieldmarshal fell. As his soul began to leave his body, the Great Bay Stallion escaped from his corral and fled past Snakeknife, making good his escape to the eastern world over the seas that flow through the great straits.

At once the Bay Stallion roared and neighed and snorted at Oceanhorse, the Great White Stallion of the East. Then Oceanhorse chomped and bowed low and raised his head and mane to meet the challenge of the Bay.

So Snakeknife lost her struggle to retain her mascot Stallion.

And Sternrider lay deepwounded near a lake where the Washerwoman had foretold his fate. As the Snakeknife and Warchariot watched him die, Sternrider rose to drink at the fresh water but could not walk as far as the way back, so he leaned upright on a large tree trunk and strapped his thick belt round him and the trunk so that he might die upright and standing. For Snakeknife and Warchariot did not dare come close for fear that he would summon up the strength to make a last lunge towards them and destroy them. But Warchariot crept closer to the dying fieldmarshal, trying to seize his throat but his heart grew faint and he and Snakeknife hesitated.

While they lurked back, Sternrider saw a cria dip down towards his head and then a crow flew down and drank the red blood as it flowed away. Then a buzzard and a hawk hovered above and Sternrider smiled a smile. He saw his life and the life of Waterbear's great eastern army summed up in one great picture of a battlefield as the four birds flew around the fallen Hillwolf. As he died, his days of youth returned when he was a fierce warrior in the field and the brightness of a true champion flashed all around him. Then the aura of his herolight returned.

And after he had died, the sword he held high in the air fell down. It stabbed the foot of Warchariot who had stepped out tentatively to try to strangle the fieldmarshal.

Then Warchariot growled, "I will kill you for your treachery."

But Warchariot never walked well again but only limped as a cripple in great pain being severely wounded by the sword of the dead Sternrider.

So Sternrider was able to strike a blow, a powerful stab against his enemies after his own life had been spent and gone.

CHAPTER TWENTY SEVEN

Ghosts of the White and the Bay

The Great Bay Stallion came to meet the Great White Stallion and the White roared up and reared and kicked his hooves. The White snorted and looked over all his herds so the Bay calmed down and did not make a challenge. The Bay realized that the war was lost and won so he drew back and galloped off to find the wild herds that rambled loose upon the moors.

So the Great Bay and the Great White led their herds separately and on peaceful plains to gallop in the warm air with honeybees and bushes and cool springs flowing through the shaded trees. Even today they gallop in the night and on the Bay's broad back there sits Sternrider and on the Great White Stallion sits Seaspear, the ghosts of warriors past and gone and lost.

Now they are no longer troubled with the ways of war - the first thing to prepare for but the last thing that you need in this short life. For there is no such thing as a won war. Only the Wallwave, only Weather wins.

Water and fire and wind and the earth plates and the grey buzzards triumph at the end, as the Wallwave and the elements sweep over the derelict camps of troops and horses.

The Great White and the Great Bay still gallop as they once did in the early days of war when they were ridden by the Seaspear and the Sternrider. But now they are dark in the moonlight, grim even in shadows.

***

Then Waterbear, at the proud prow of his ship, returned to his eastern kingdom and his throne high on the stone fastness by the sea. There with Queen Springvision and his four fieldmarshals with their four queens they ruled the Wavewarriors.

Now they were no longer threatened by Snakeknife and Warchariot who joined the Four Witches of Kill and the Mooncrow, retreating into the shadows of their caves, muttering and sneering among their spells and visions.

For many years the Hillwolves of the West made no attempt to snare or plot against the Wavewarriors of the East, until the Hillwolves once again became restless and revived the old jealousies and ambitions so that they once more made plots against the Waterbear. The years of waves swept over the long oceans as peaceful seas rolled on — only the storms of weather, not of men, interrupted the world until the boy Wallwave became fully trained as a Wavewarrior champion.

Then the Four Witches of Kill began to plot again so giving rise to the strange adventures which are told in the many tales and fantasies of Wallwave the rising son of the empire of the East.

The End